I0780148

LOVED AND LOST

By
Janeen Swart

This book is a work of fiction. Names,
characters, dates, places, dates, incidents and
dialogues are either products of the author's
imagination or used fictitiously. Any resemblance to
actual persons, living or dead, or events is
coincidental.

LOVED AND LOST is very loosely patterned
after the life of Jennie Conrad. As I looked for a
woman to emulate for this historical novel about the
settlement of northwestern Indiana, Jennie's life came
forward as an interesting female character to use as a
pattern for my story.

Many of the dates of her life and some of the
historical events that she was involved with are
similar. However, most of the events are completely
fictitious and in no way are they meant to be an
account of Jennie Conrad's life.

ISBN: 978-1-965352-68-7

Prologue: 1861

The half-moon shed a sliver of light, and a glimmer of the lake's surface shimmering in the distance emerged between the dense cover of oaks. Within this vast expanse of water known as Willow Lake, arose the stronghold known as Refuge Island, a patch of land several acres in extent, well covered with scrub-oak and sand dunes and edged by a dense growth of cattails and wild rice. Because deep water surrounded this island, a surprise attack by officers of the law was almost impossible. But for the bandits who wanted to remain isolated, entering and exiting this island home was familiar, even with its difficult to negotiate paths.

From the west, winding, murky 'hog-back' trails lying close to the surface of the lake but obscured by the water, zigzagged toward the hideout on Refuge Island. This means of entrance made a much easier route than swimming one's horse through the deep waters surrounding the island. The tricky part became finding the rudimentary corduroy roadway where the 'hog-back' stopped. Criminals masterfully used this means to finish their trek of three to four hundred feet into their secure haven on Refuge Island, using this secret submerged trail of logs.

In the cover of darkness, it's to this island that Mike Shatner and two of his trusted men made their way on horseback after a productive day of plunder, their gunny sacks now full of real currency and a few gold pieces. Several days previous, they had departed with their sacks of stolen goods taken from unsuspecting highwaymen over the past months. Spreading out through the countryside, each of the outlaws sold the items to those looking for bargains, sometimes to the same people who had their items stolen. Now, moving with measured steps in the semi-darkness, they picked their way from the west through the marsh trail.

"Keep up now," hissed Shatner, his gruff voice making it almost impossible to whisper. "Stay close and quiet. The hogbacks are just ahead."

Wade, the second rider following behind Shatner and a much smaller man, turned with a slight nod to Ned who followed close behind him, the meaning being no more talking until we get to the shack.

The three horses, accustomed to walking through the low swampy water, stomped along with careful precision. The sound of their hooves entering and lifting through the water and the occasional bird or animal call became the only sounds heard after Mike's command.

Wade McCallen joined up with Shatner when he witnessed old Shatner using his long knife to persuade some unlikely travelers to hand over their money belts. After pulling his knife from the body, Shatner wiped the blood off his knife on the victim's clothes, looked up at Wade and asked, "You good with a knife? I don't use guns; don't like the noise they make. Knives are my weapon of choice if need be."

"Yes, sir. I can use a knife right well."

Shatner nodded, accepting Wade's answer and the deal was sealed. Wade had ridden with Shatner ever since, raiding travelers to hand over their merchandise. He liked Shatner's rough demeanor and his competence in thievery, even though he didn't trust him as far as he could throw him.

Living at Refuge Island gave little chance for a change of clothes or washing up, so the gang's wild look put fear into their victims and scared them into compliance even before they drew their knives. Most handed over their goods without protest. Today, selling their plunder had brought in a good haul of cash and some gold, but Wade was exhausted from riding from town-to-town selling the stolen goods. Relaxing with a game of cards and some liquor would be a well-needed reward.

Keeping a watchful eye behind the trio was Ned's job as the last rider. His slender, young body turned first to the right, followed by four steps of the horse, then turning to the left for another count of four. Shatner had recruited Ned as an added gang member after he witnessed his quick ambush and thievery of a traveler on the road to Kankakee. Now while riding with Shatner, Ned seldom worried about the future, just his boss's occasional mad outbursts that made him want to run. Shatner's temper could erupt at any moment.

The familiar smell of a wood fire filled the air as the men rode further and before long the small crudely built cabin came into view. Made with unpeeled logs and without a foundation, the cabin gave the impression it would tilt over at any moment, but it served the purpose of a place to pull back and rest.

Shatner pulled up twenty feet from the scene, held up his hand and stopped to listen. When only the sounds of men sparring over cards hit their ears, Shatner clicked his horse to continue forward to the clearing near the cabin. Climbing down from his mount, Shatner barked, "Ned, get the horses unsaddled and tied off. Meet us out back of the cabin. We'll sort out our take for the day."

Without delay, never quite trusting his companions, Ned hurried to complete his job and get back to dispensing the loot. He grabbed the horses' bridles and led them to a 'hillside stable,' dug out of the side of a sand dune. Sweeping away some of the brush used to conceal the opening, Ned led the horses inside, unsaddled them, and tied them to the rope strung across the makeshift stable. He'd go back later to feed and water them.

Light from within the cabin spilled from the half door when Ned joined the other two outlaws. The money and gold coins from their pillage were already spread out on a huge oak stump behind the cabin.

"All I want is the gold. You boys can divide up the rest. I know you want to get in that poker game," said Shatner. He grabbed the five gold coins. "I gotta take a piss."

Shatner walked toward a wooded area away from the clearing around the cabin. Wade and Ned watched him for a bit, then counted out the paper money and divided it equally.

Ned took his half and stashed it into his shirt pocket. "I heard Old Shatner has a nail keg out there somewhere. He always makes an excuse to leave as soon as he takes his share. He must stash his gold in that nail keg every time we get back here. I'd sure like to follow him one day to see where he goes, but he wouldn't have any qualms about ambushing me and sticking that big knife of his into this skinny body."

Wade nodded. "Yep, you better not try it, not if you want to keep that hide on you."

The two fellow marauders entered the cabin. Seated around a large table in the center of the one room were another four grubby looking men. An oil lamp set to one side gave enough light for the participants to see their cards and watch for cheating hands. A fire roared in the crude fireplace cut out of a section of the wall, with a mud and stick chimney built outside the cabin to vent the smoke.

"Come on in, boys, and join us," said Black Jake. "We need some fresh bait."

Ned and Wade grabbed a couple wood blocks to use for chairs and sidled up to the table, waiting to join in on the next hand.

"Where's your boss?" asked John Stevens, trying to clear his smoke damaged voice. A lengthy coughing spell exploded from his throat, afterwards spitting on the floor of the cabin.

"Had to take a piss," said Wade, catching the eyes of the men at the table.

"Yeah, we know his habits," added Jake. "He'll be richer than all of us put together some day, if he lives that long, if you know what I mean."

Guffaws and knee slaps circled round the group. Quiet returned. Only the night sounds of frogs croaking, the occasional coyote call and the hoot of an owl broke the stillness all around the poker table.

After another round of play, Shatner stumbled into the cabin, his clothes covered with blood. Always reserved around old Shatner, the men stared without questioning.

"Got part of a deer carcass that needs trimming and cooked. Had to fight off and kill the coyote who downed it," announced Mike. "Get out there and gut it, if you want to eat."

Later the outlaws feasted on venison and eventually turned in for the night.

~

The posse positioned themselves to surround the cabin and each man hid behind a large oak for cover with gun cocked and ready. Someone lit a lantern and sounds of men rustling inside the cabin alerted the men who waited in the dark. Muffled voices passed through the night air into the twilight.

"You men come out of there with your hands up," called Sheriff Baum. He and twelve other men, including Jake Bushionberry, Allen Whitman, Henry Riley and his hired hand Isom, all new to the area around Refuge Island, had tracked Shatner and his men for miles at quite a distance behind. Once they neared the outlaws' cabin, they had bided their time until just before dawn hoping to surprise the group while sleeping.

A shot rang out from inside the cabin.

The posse waited. No one appeared at the doorways. Sheriff Baum called out again, "Come out and drop your weapons."

More shots came from inside the cabin. The sheriff fired the first shot from outside, and all hell broke loose. The posse punctured the cabin with a barrage of bullets for nearly ten minutes. When the noise died down, two men appeared with hands in the air.

"Hold your fire," yelled the sheriff. He and his men moved forward. "Anybody else in there?"

"The rest are dead or wounded," yelled Wade, holding his head where a bullet had grazed his scalp.

Securing both men who surrendered, Sheriff Baum and his men helped themselves to what little food and drink the outlaws had stashed and settled in to wait for daylight. At first light, they confiscated the cash they found on each bandit and loaded the bodies on the bandits' horses for transport back to Momence. Mike Shatner was identified as one of the victims of the bullet barrage. The men found no cash on his body, just a long hunter's knife, wiped clean.

Chapter 1: 1938

The sun beat down on Bailey as she walked. The warm, humid July weather made the walk to the store a tiresome inconvenience. She wiped the sweat from her forehead as she made her trek to Robinsons' General Store. Her ankle-length skirt and long-sleeved blouse added to her discomfort. The dust swirled up into her eyes each time the wind picked up. Wisps of her long chestnut hair swirled into her face and remain glued there by the beads of sweat forming on her brow.

Bailey had made this walk more often since her Great Aunt Josie moved in with them several months ago. Her husband, John, complained to her about the situation in private, but what could she do? Aunt Josie had no one else to care for her. If they didn't take her in, she'd be all alone and Bailey couldn't bear to think of her aunt not having any family to visit with and care for her needs.

The old lady had made a fortune in her lifetime but now she needed looking after, both physically and financially. Bailey didn't care about the rumors of Aunt Josie's gold, or money or the promise of an inheritance. She truly wanted to help out by giving Josie a loving home in her final days. Bailey had always been curious about Aunt Josie's life. Though she and her family had never spent time with her, Bailey's parents had told many stories about Aunt Josie. Bailey wanted to hear more. Besides enjoying her aunt's company, Bailey hoped to get her to open up about her experiences. If she could get her to agree, Bailey planned to write about Aunt Josie's life in a series for the newspaper. Writing free-lance stories for the Indianapolis Star would give Bailey a little extra cash to add to John's income. His business as veterinarian here in town had just taken off, but some couldn't afford to pay so John sometimes took barter items for payment.

Their home and John's office, located a few blocks out of town, made for a pleasant walk when the weather cooperated, but not today. The heat made her walk slower by the minute. Various businesses lined either side of the small downtown. Bailey passed the dime store which also offered an ice cream counter, the small café, the local post office and a modest millinery shop as she trudged along. Similar shops filled the opposite side, and shoppers called out greetings to one another and to Bailey.

When she reached Robinson's, Bailey revived a little and hurried up the steps. The familiar smell of fresh ground coffee combined with musty old shelves and sweet penny candy welcomed Bailey as she pulled open the heavy wood and glass door that led into the general store. A little bell above the door tinkled when she tugged it open.

Walking into the store, Bailey called out, "Hello Harold. How are you today? Hot day out there. Did the typing paper come in?"

Harold looked up from his work of stacking the shelves and nodded. He wore an apron that covered his white shirt and dark pants just in case he'd need to cut some meat from the cold locker or dig into a barrel of potatoes for a customer. Tiny beads of sweat caused his wire-rimmed glasses to fall to the tip of his nose. He pushed them up and ran his hand over his nearly bald head as if still trying to straighten a few strands of hair.

"Hi, Bailey. Hot in here too. Hot all over. Yep, paper came in. It's on the back shelf."

The old wooden floorboards creaked and bent somewhat in spots as Bailey headed for the back of the store where Harold Robinson kept the paper supplies for sale. She'd need plenty of typewriter paper if she was going to give her stories a professional look. She grabbed the cheapest box of paper Mr. Robinson had on the shelf. It would have to do since she was trying to make money, not spend it. Heading up and down the aisles, she gathered a few more items and placed them in her basket. Stopping every couple of feet, she scanned the shelves, so she wouldn't forget anything they'd need for the next couple of days. She didn't want to make another trip to the store in the heat if she didn't have to.

The hum of voices became louder the closer she got to the register. Local men hung out at the table near the front of the store where in winter, a fire crackled in the corner from the pot-bellied stove. Drinking coffee and sharing stories, they often talked about the events and the residents in their small town. Bailey stopped short when she heard one of the men say her Aunt Josie's name.

"Josie Morris? Humph! That old battleaxe sure was a mean one in her day. She would chase the kids who were picking berries off her property with a whip. Bailey is going to have her hands full."

Bailey's breath caught. Her head felt like a tiny hammer pounded on the inside of her skull.

"I heard a story about Josie that she rode around the boundaries of her property in a buggy with a shotgun across her lap. She sure tried to keep anybody from trespassing," added another voice.

The men grunted in agreement. Then one more coffee drinker added, "I wouldn't want to have to deal with her. Bailey and John will be ready to send her packing after a month, mark my words."

A loud crash came from the aisle next to Bailey. "Oww! Dang those canned beans. Never could stack them very well. Now my toe will be throbbing all day."

Bailey hurried around the corner of the aisle and saw Mr. Robinson, his red bowtie disheveled, still holding two cans of beans. Several other cans had fallen and rolled across the slanting floor toward the opposite aisle.

Bailey hurried to help. Picking up the cans and placing on the shelf, she whispered, "Thanks for the distraction. Those men sure don't like my great aunt. Do you think those stories are true?"

"Everyone's got an opinion now days. Those guys are going by hearsay. They don't have firsthand knowledge of what Josie did or didn't do. I'd say you better talk to your aunt and see if she can shed some light on some of those stories." He placed the cans he held back on the shelf. "Ready to check out?"

The men sat in silence around the table as Harold checked out the items Bailey needed to purchase. He bagged them up for her, being careful with the box of typewriter paper. Bailey paid her bill without looking toward the table of men. She headed toward the door to leave but then thought better of it. She walked back to the coffee group. Tears stung her eyes as she stood a moment and stared at the men one at a time. "Sticks and stones."

"Aww, we didn't mean anything by what we said," offered Nate Stilley. The other guys nodded their heads in agreement.

She turned and strode toward the door. Walking out of the store, a smile formed on her lips. She just wanted those men to know she had heard their gossip. But it wasn't the first time Bailey heard stories about Aunt Josie's wild side. Most of the people living in the nearest town to where Josie grew up had bad feelings toward her and Bailey's parents had told some of those same stories, but they had always tried to put them in a better light. Maybe Bailey could change people's opinions if she could get Aunt Josie to let her write her life story for the newspaper.

Walking as fast as the heat would allow, she bounded up the front porch steps and into their house. Placing the basket of items she bought on the kitchen table, Bailey hurried in to check on her aunt. The scene could have made a picture postcard. Josie was seated near an open window in the parlor, listening to the radio and stitching a lovely piece of embroidery. She had pulled her gray hair away from her face and tied it into a loose bun toward the top of her head, allowing whisps of curls to fall loosely around her round face. She wore a pearl necklace that hung just above the neckline of her dark taffeta dress.

Josie laid her embroidery down when she saw Bailey. "My goodness, child, what has come over you? You look like you're ready to skin a polecat."

Bailey wiped at her face. The tears had mixed with the beads of sweat making streaks down each cheek. "I don't understand how you can be so sweet to me and others think you're a mean, nasty old woman." She flopped down on the chair next to Josie.

"Are those gossips going on about me again?" Josie smiled. "Just sit here and cool off, girl. You've gotten yourself all worked up. Don't let yourself get upset about what people say about me. Their whispered words aren't exactly soaked with the complete truth."

Bailey moved to the footstool in front of her aunt, the warm summer breeze coming through the window, drying the ringlets around her face. She sighed and looked up at her dear aunt who smiled back at her. How could anyone think this sweet old woman had been such a nasty character?

Before Bailey had a chance to think about how she wanted to ask, her words spilled out. "Would you be willing to tell me the story of your life? We could help each other out if you would. I can make some extra money by publishing them and the stories will make people understand the truth about you."

Josie looked out the window as if she was staring across the years. Her smile faded and lines formed across her brow. She held that pose for several minutes, then said, "I'm not so sure you want to hear the truth, dear. I'm afraid in some ways, they may be right. I wasn't a very nice person at times. But if you think it will help you and John with paying for having me stay here with you, I'll do it on one condition; we don't use my true name. Your readers will probably figure out who it is your writing about, but I'm only here for this world a short time yet, and I don't want people talking about me any more than they already are."

Bailey jumped up and hugged her aunt. "You won't be sorry. Let me grab a pencil and paper."

Laughing, Aunt Josie sat back and laid her embroidery on the lamp table. When Bailey returned, she asked, "What do you want to know?"

"Let's start from the beginning. When were you born and how did you end up in Rensselaer?"

"I guess that's a good place to start. I was born in 1856 to Henry and Margaret Riley. My father was one of the posse that brought down the outlaw, Mike Shatner. My parents lived near the town of Momence in Illinois. The people there were tired of Shatner's gang terrorizing the roads and robbing the travelers. They put together a posse and followed Mike and his men over into Indiana and raided their hideout on Refuge Island."

The afternoon sun shone through the window making the house unbearably warm, but Bailey could only think about taking notes and writing this story, forgetting about the dinner she needed to prepare.

Chapter 2

Bailey got comfortable as she sat by the dining table near her aunt with her pencil poised.

"I need to write all this down if I'm going to be able to write a good story. So, did your parents always live here in Indiana?"

Beginnings, 1850's

While my grandmother was too busy with the work of the homestead to give the children attention, my mother's younger siblings depended on her. Being the oldest, she became the substitute parent, but she often daydreamed about escaping to somewhere else.

"Maggie, I'm hungry," cried her sister, Penny.

"Take me with you to the outhouse, Maggie. I'm scared to go in the dark," begged little Sharon.

Margaret's nerves couldn't take much more, so she welcomed the diversion that Henry provided. She looked forward to his visits more each day.

"Henry's here, again, Maggie," yelled her twelve-year-old brother, James. In a quieter tone he added, "He looks too old for you."

Magaret didn't care if Henry was quite a bit older and not particularly handsome. His red hair and beard, and pale complexion didn't make him very desirable to look at, but he already owned several tracts of property and seemed to be on his way to success. She jumped at the chance to leave her life behind when he asked her father for her hand in marriage.

However, once they were married, Margaret found out much of

the land Henry owned for farming could not support them. Any crops Henry planted dried too quickly on the sandy Ohio soil. The land just wasn't producing like they had hoped, and Henry had to work as a schoolteacher part of the year just to make ends meet. The family's prospects for making their farm a success became gloomier as the months passed, especially after Henry fell sick the second winter and couldn't teach. The newlyweds soon got fed up with farming the unpredictable land they owned in Ohio. Being an educated man, my father hoped to be able to manage, not do actual work with his hands. They began to look for new options for making a living.

My parents heard through traveling relatives about property further west available to homestead with the chance to purchase. With Mother's drive and ambition, and Father's entrepreneurial nature, they decided to take the plunge, sell all they had and make the move. The National Road had been completed to Indiana in the early 1850's, so Henry and Margaret decided to follow the road to Indianapolis and then west to St. Louis and beyond.

The hard part came when Henry had to explain his plan to his father-in-law. James Dawson, my grandfather, who was a proud and unyielding man. When my father confronted him to explain their plan, he stood listening with his arms folded across his huge barrel chest. Standing a foot taller than my father, he stared down at Henry's uplifted face with his dark, brooding eyes.

Henry's voice wavered. "Margaret and I have decided to move west. When we get to Indianapolis, we'll winter at my Uncle Jeremiah's. After the spring thaw, we'll head further west to find land to homestead."

"I don't like that idea at all, Henry. Margaret's mother won't like the fact that she'll be moving so far away from us."

My father feigned sympathy, but the next day he continued with their plans and bought a large wagon and team of oxen. With Margaret's ability to sway her father into just about anything, my grandfather agreed to bless the move and even gave the young couple extra cash for their trip and settlement of a homestead. Margaret, now in her early months of pregnancy, did not divulge that information to her parents for fear they would stop their endeavor.

My mother didn't want to do without any of the luxuries she'd become accustomed to, so Henry procured a wagon nearly large enough for all her treasures. She packed spooled bedspreads, feather mattresses, a walnut bureau, a China service, silverware and even dainty glassware. And Henry was just as bad. He had to have boxes of books and his organ. Last came the necessities like bags of flour, sacks of coffee and sugar and beans. Add to that, the axes, hammers, rifles and shot needed for protection. Once all was loaded, the wagon resembled a small mountain. An extra set of oxen had to be added to pull the heavy load.

At first a somewhat holiday feeling must have characterized my parents' journey along with the others in the small wagon train. Making camp along the road, once Henry had the fire started, Mom cooked over the open flame and enjoyed the conversations with fellow travelers. Her jovial nature became a magnet for all who wanted to socialize. A group almost always gathered around their campfire.

One of the men standing near the fire shared his thoughts. "Only a couple more days till we get to the big city. Think you'll be able to wait until then to have that little one?"

"What makes you think I'm going to have a baby, sir? Perhaps this is all my body under these frocks." At that point, my mother opened wide her arms for all to see her girth. Her loud laugh resonated around the fire while slapping the fellow's back and nearly knocking him into the blaze.

Henry glared at her and walked to the back of the wagon to climb in for the night. Seeing his reaction, Mom soon followed. The last thing she ever wanted to do was to hurt my dad. Although small in stature, he was her rock, her balance wheel. Margaret called out, "Don't go getting all upset, Henry. You know you're the only man for me." Her laugh could be heard as far back as the fire.

My father opened his arms to welcome her, then helped her climb into their wagon for the night. They never could stay angry with one another for very long.

While on the trail, Henry overheard some of their fellow travelers talking. "There's land over there in northwest Indiana that hasn't been tamed. Good fertile bottom land lying south of that river that floods every spring. They say the whole area is teeming with wildlife, too."

That was all my father needed to hear. He discussed the change of plans to go north instead of west with my mother. They could take the newly completed Michigan Road to Michigan City then follow rough-hewn roads to the area the men had mentioned. Margaret liked the idea of staying closer to civilization. The trip farther west into the plains appeared endless, and she was ready to settle down.

The wagon group swayed and bumped along, with each day seeming longer than the last, especially for Margaret who was getting closer to her due date. Late one day in October, they finally pulled up to the covered bridge that crossed the White River into Indianapolis. Henry climbed down from the wagon to check their load before crossing.

A bystander shook his head in disbelief. "Where you headed?"

"Eventually going to homestead up north."

Laughing, the guy continued, "Man, you aren't going to need half of what you're hauling in that wagon when you get where you're going."

Mom's broad smile could charm almost anyone, and her lovely dark brown hair framing her gentle face made her a favorite among the travelers. From high up on the wagon seat Mother insisted, "I need my linens, my bureau and that fine cook stove. I'll have you know; we've come this far; we'll make it to our destination just fine."

The man smiled and scratched his chin, shook his head and walked on.

Once over that narrow-covered bridge, the group of wagons made camp in the grassy area along the river. The nearly full moon shed a canopy of dim light over the travelers. Shadows moved inside each wagon until the group settled in for a long-needed respite. But after several hours, Margaret's screams of pain slashed through the stillness of the night. "The baby's coming."

Henry sat holding Margaret's hand for the long hours of her delivery. By morning it was obvious that something was terribly wrong. Dog-tired, Mother pushed one last time. A tiny blue baby finally expelled into Henry's hands with no loud cries cutting through the evening stillness.

Distressed, Mother refused to look at the small lifeless form. "Take it away."

Dad wrapped the tiny infant in a blanket and buried the bundle in the soft dirt along the river, marking the grave with a few stones he collected. Margaret never asked, and he never explained what he did. The next day the young couple found a winter home with Henry's Uncle Jeremiah. Mother needed the rest and Henry used the months to work as a tutor to add to their nest egg.

In the spring, they left as soon as the roads and paths were clear of snow. They again moved their overloaded wagon north and did indeed find fertile land just south of the Kankakee River in Beaver County in northwest Indiana. They selected a permanent homestead site in a secluded area and began building their home.

~

Since the homestead was far from any town, when they needed supplies, they made the trip to the nearest town together. Margaret spent her time buying items at the general store while Dad joined the men in the local saloon. He loved a good deal and before Mother knew what he had done, Henry had agreed to one of the best deals he ever made.

When he entered the saloon, his attention was drawn immediately to a large man who sat at a table facing the door of the establishment. The man wore a fine black suit and on his head was an equally fine black bowler hat. A huge cigar hung from his mouth although it didn't appear to be lit. When he spoke, the cigar bounced up and down like a jack rabbit. Several men sat around the table with him, and many others stood intermingling in the area around the table. My father's curiosity became too much for him to stand back. He walked closer, keeping an ear out for what the man proposed.

The guy continued his loud rant keeping an eye toward the newcomer as Henry walked forward. "It's 1852, by God, and there's going to be a great need for timber before long. A man can make a considerable profit by buying up the timber lands around here. My benefactor, Col. Samuel Powell, of New York has sent me to solicit partners in this noble endeavor. I need just one person willing to partner with the Colonel. Do I have any brave person willing to put his money into this great investment?"

Most of the men backed off or fell silent, having no money to spend, but Henry had the extra cash his father-in-law had gifted them. Without much thought and without consulting Margaret he called out, "I'll take you up on your offer."

Papers were signed within the half-hour. Afterwards, Henry had one drink to seal the deal with the big man and then headed out to find Margaret. With the excitement of a schoolboy, he spilled his plan to her, but her puckered brows and downturned lips gave him cause to reign in his enthusiasm.

My father reached for Mother's hand and promised. "Don't worry. When all those settlers come into this prairie, these timber lands will become very profitable. We'll get a hundred-fold return on your dad's money."

Mom's lips turned up at the corners like a slow-moving caterpillar. "I trust your judgement, Henry, but I wish you would have included me in the excitement. You know I love to be part of the action."

True to his words, my parents continued to expand their holdings. Their agricultural pursuits and Dad's financial investments were all paying good dividends, so when Col. Powell died in 1853, they bought out the interests of Powell's sons and widow, an estate totaling one thousand three hundred twenty acres. The name of their property was changed to Riley's Grove. Three years later, Margaret delivered a healthy baby, and they named her, Josie. I became the reason, Henry and Margaret continued to build their empire.

Henry built a flourishing cattle business, eventually raising and selling his own animals, rather than purchasing them from other producers. When it came to his cattle business, my father seemed to always find a way to come out on top. On a Sunday in early autumn, 1858, citizens of Chicago in the neighborhood of State Street beheld the unusual spectacle of a herd of one hundred eighty-five head of cattle being driven north through that thoroughfare. Dad had driven his herd from his farm in Beaver County to the Chicago market. However, once there, he was unable to find a buyer for the cattle, so the stock was slaughtered, and the meat sold right there on the spot. The butchering of the cattle was done in a large open field located west of State Street and Randolph Street.

The Civil War began in the 1860's, and the Riley's were able to realize high prices caused by wartime shortages. So, when President Lincoln, now a good friend of my father's, needed supplies for the war, they equipped a complete mounted regiment at their own expense.

As a result of their fiscal abundance, my early years on the frontier became a mixture of wealth and an unconventional upbringing. My parents doted on me but still expected me to do my part on the homestead. I, in turn, tried to learn everything I could from both of my parents and the many visitors who frequented Riley's Grove.

Chapter 3

Is your hand getting tired, dear? I know I've been rambling for quite a while."

Bailey looked out the window where daylight was turning to dusk. John would be home soon. "I hate to quit, but I need to get dinner started. Let's work again after breakfast tomorrow."

But the next morning, John needed Bailey to accompany him on a call to a farm nearby to vaccinate the cattle there against Black Leg. So, she and Aunt Josie couldn't work again until after lunch and then Josie kept nodding off. Finally in the middle of the afternoon, Josie continued her tale.

1857-1861

My family, much like the rest of Riley's Grove area residents, developed our own unique code of ethics based on trust and the Robin Hood principle, which fit within our lifestyles and beliefs. Basically, my parents and the other settlers didn't question anybody's way of living as long as everyone behaved within the somewhat obscured fringes of the law. That's just the way things were on the frontier.

Travelers often stopped for a night's boarding at Riley's Grove, some on their way to Willow Lake. Leroy Paine furnished transportation from Kankakee to the lake for twelve dollars where the hunting was plentiful. Mom never turned anyone away. My friendliness made me a favorite of the travelers. As a small child, I had curly hair, the color of a copper penny, much like my father's, not like the grey you see now. My fair skin, liberally sprinkled with freckles, drew compliments from guests. I loved to sit by their side as they told stories of their travels. I would question them until they ran out of tales. My favorite stories were about the explorers who found gold out west.

I'd ask the same question of each visitor. "Do you think I'll be able to find gold out west someday?"

They would laugh and say I was too young to worry about leaving home, but I kept asking and dreaming of finding gold someday.

As I grew up, my mother tried to tame my precocious ways into well-mannered poise and gracefulness. She also instilled in me the same character traits she possessed; her ability to control, her invincibility, her strong will, and her well-controlled but volcanic temper. From my father I inherited an uncompromising attitude and the drive to keep expanding my holdings.

Because of my frontier upbringing, I learned the skills of riding, roping, shooting, and cattle raising. I contributed to the household chores, but they were never my favorite. Once these duties were complete, I was free to play in the area surrounding the homestead; hunting, fishing and exploring. Often, I'd ride to the edge of the wide lake near our home. Willow Lake was so shallow; you could walk across most areas, and I often tried to in the summer months. I loved to sit and watch the ducks and geese land in the fall, and I kept my eye out for small mammals I could shoot to bring home for dinner.

Although there had been some attempts by the State of Indiana to drain the big body of water known as Willow Lake by digging a ditch to connect the lake to the Kankakee River, the process of draining the lake wasn't very successful. It only succeeded in causing the shoreline to recede ten feet, which made for a better playground. Sometimes I would wade in shallow water or play on the sandy shore making sand shapes. Being intimate with and dependent on nature taught me to be resourceful and later I used those traits in my business dealings and farming techniques.

Having few friends my age to play with, my companions were cowboys and my parents' acquaintances who frequented Riley's Grove. Our ranch hands weren't just workers. Mother also welcomed them into our family circle. She made sure their bunk house was comfortable, and the food prepared by Mrs. Jaynes, who worked for us, was the best in the area. If the cowhand liked to read, my father's books were available to the men.

The ranch hands often spent their free time entertaining me and I loved the attention. I would call out, "Time for a ride," and one or another of the men would bend at the waist and I enjoyed a bucking contest where the unlucky cowboy did his best to throw me off.

Our family was blessed for many years because one unemployed cowhand rode into the Riley homestead looking for a meal. With his dark-skinned body, he stood apart from the rest of the hands, standing arrow straight and riding in the same way. His beaded leather clothing made him look like a warrior. As year went by, Isom became almost a member of our family. He even tried his hand at cooking an evening meal occasionally. I never tired of sitting by his side in the evenings.

"Play me a song, Isom."

Isom entertained us with song after song on either his fiddle or mouth harp, both at which he was a master. His talents came in handy at the events Margaret often planned.

Mother loved to entertain, and my parents hosted many dances that often lasted till dawn. My dad's organ playing became the center of the celebration. Guns were checked at the door and drinking was done only in the barn. The men dressed in dark suits with vests, and white shirts with stiff starched collars. Mustaches had to be waxed and curled. The women wore dresses with tight fitting bodices and long, flowing skirts. Their hair was done on top of their head, either in a French twist or a bun with bangs curled to a frizz.

I was allowed to join in all these activities. Wearing my best dress and with ribbons in my long hair, I joined the group of partygoers who danced away the night. My parents never sheltered me or kept me from the adults, but often I dropped off to sleep on the hay before the end of the party.

Isom would notice me and ask, "Want me to carry her to bed, Missus Riley? She looks plum tuckered out." He would pick me up with the care of a mother cat carrying a kitten and deposit me in my bed without me realizing I had been moved.

Christmas was another time everyone looked forward to. My mother celebrated Christmas as well as the frontier allowed, baking pies and cookies, and making candy and popcorn. Several days before Christmas she would ask if I wanted to help make decorations for the cabin.

I'd jump from my chair in excitement. "When can we string the berries, we dried?"

Mother would pull down the sack with the dried berries and show me how to thread the needle used to puncture each berry, then slide it down the string. Always a quick learner, before long, I'd exclaim. "Look, my string is filled. Show me how to tie the knot so the berries will stay on the string."

While I worked stringing the berries, Mother sang as she would string pinecones to add to the evergreen boughs she hung above the doors. Early on Christmas Eve we'd make a trek to the woods to find a pine tree to bring in to decorate.

With no church building within driving distance, all present on the homestead would gather around our hearth later on Christmas Eve. Dad would do his best impression of a pastor. "I'll be reading the Christmas story from Luke 2 from God's word. 'In those days Caesar Augustus issued a decree that a census should be taken of the entire Roman world. This was the first census that took place while Quirinius was governor of Syria'. . .."

Isom then played Christmas carols, ending with a soulful rendition of 'Silent Night.'

With no school close to our homestead, my father taught me reading lessons from the Bible, Shakespeare, Emerson, and Sir Walter Scott. With the extensive number of books Dad brought with him to our new home, I never lacked in choices for reading. Mother took over where numbers were concerned. Often, she enlisted my help in figuring out long lists of numbers to keep the household records and I loved dealing with the accounts. Something I never tired of as I expanded my businesses.

Fear struck our household late one evening in October of 1861, when a large group of men rode up to our homestead. A sheen covered their horses from hard and fast riding. A large man dressed in buckskin and wearing a wide-brimmed hat, dismounted, but the others remained on their horses, ready to move on.

Father left the cabin to greet the men. "Hello, Sheriff. What brings you all the way from Momence at this late hour?"

Sherrif Brendon moved closer to shake Father's outstretched hand. "We're going after Shatner and his gang. Getting tired of his marauding in these parts. Thought maybe you could join us. We need someone to lead us into that lake to the island where they're holed up."

At that moment, Mother joined my father in front of our home and heard the sheriff's request. "Take Isom with you, too. He'll be better at tracking their movements."

Nodding his head in approval, my father headed to the barn to saddle his horse and wake Isom. I suspected Mother didn't think Dad could handle leading the posse into the lake and she knew Isom would do his best to bring him back home.

That whole night, Mom sat by the fire waiting for any sound of the riders returning. I'm sure her thoughts were churning with wild scenes of bloody events. She finally fell asleep there in the rocking chair with me wrapped in a blanket by her side.

"Mommy, I'm hungry." I stood beside the chair staring into my mother's half-opened eyes.

As she prepared the morning meal, we kept our ears tuned to any sound that might indicate the posse had returned. Finally mid-morning, the welcome sound of hooves on the hardened path leading to the bunkhouse came through to our ears, changing our worry into relief.

"What happened? Tell me all about it." Mom's breathless voice greeted the men. She had run the few yards to the bunkhouse holding me in her arms. "Come on into the cabin and have some breakfast, all of you."

Sherriff Brendon dismounted and started to lead his horse toward the water trough. "Much obliged, Mrs. Riley, but we'll just give our horses a drink and be on our way. We've got to get these wounded to the Doc and the rest locked up."

My eyes scanned the posse. Until Sheriff Baum answered, I hadn't noticed the extra riders. Dad and Isom attended to their horses while the rest of the posse walked theirs to the water trough. Mom shook as she held me tight. When Dad joined us, she asked again, "What happened?"

He glanced at me and shook his head slightly. "Nothing much. We found the outlaw's cabin, and some of the outlaws got taken alive."

Later that morning, while I played on the porch with the kittens, I heard Dad share more. "It was a bloodbath. I don't want to ever see anything like that again, but Sheriff Baum said it had to be done. We confiscated all the cash the outlaws had, but it didn't come close to what should have been there. The sheriff used some rough tactics to persuade one of the outlaws to divulge the fact that Shatner always took the gold and buried it somewhere on Refuge Island. Unfortunately, Shatner was one of the casualties, so there's no one that can explain where the gold is buried."

Margaret gasped. "So, that gold could be ours if we can find it since its on our property."

I couldn't contain my excitement. I opened the door and shrieked, "Buried treasure? I'm going to find it someday."

I'll never forget my parents' look of shock when they saw me standing in the doorway smiling as wide as the lantern light.

~

Aunt Josie began to laugh so loud she even snorted. Bailey couldn't help but laugh, too. She and Josie had tears running down their cheeks when John walked in.

"What's so funny?" John handed his handkerchief to Bailey. "Are you okay?"

Bailey could only nod.

Wiping her eyes with her own hanky, Aunt Josie said, "I was so silly in those days. I really believed there was buried treasure on my property. I let it make me into a nasty old lady at times because I always thought someone was trying to steal from me."

"Just wait until I can publish these stories, people will have a different opinion, I'm sure."

John's wide-eyed face and the okay sign he made from behind Aunt Josie nearly made Bailey burst out laughing again.

Chapter 4: 1870-1873

My parents' move to Indiana proved to be a lucrative arrangement. Dad continued to expand his land holdings and at one time owned over twenty-five thousand acres of land in Illinois and Indiana. He and Mother specialized in raising Hereford cattle and Percheron horses. They also opened a general store in Momence and later an ice harvesting company in Kankakee. As time went on, Henry diversified into other enterprises. In 1868, he constructed a "combination store" in Chebanse, on the northwest corner of Chebanse Avenue and Chestnut Street. The two-story building, claimed to be the largest building between Chicago and Danville. It housed nine stores, a bank, newspaper office, and a barbershop.

Thankfully most of Dad's building was completed before the Chicago fire. After 1871, the swamp's timber resources were overly exploited and after the fire, lumber was more difficult to find. Large red and white oaks, beeches, and maple trees were cut down and sent to Chicago to rebuild the city. Timber thievery became a regular occurrence, and steamboats chugged up and down the river delivering the logs, fenceposts and raw lumber on rafts pulled behind the boats.

Dad had another ambitious undertaking to occupy his time. He began focusing on the draining of Willow Lake just south of the Kankakee River in Indiana. This would add another five thousand usable acres to his holdings. When he presented the proposal to the state, the move was rejected at first, with the state arguing that they had only sold the shoreline to the lake and not the entire property. Dad was not a man to be deterred. He had his attorney file a lawsuit and in Indiana vs. Riley, the Indiana Supreme Court ruled that the state also sold the land under the lake in the transaction.

When my father returned from Indianapolis to share his news, he grabbed me and swung me around. "Your daddy's going to dig the biggest ditch you've ever seen and get us more land for our farm."

Pushing back my auburn curls that had fallen down into my face, I clapped my hands with excitement. "Maybe after the water is gone, I'll be able to find the gold."

My parents stared at me and then looked at one another. Dad rubbed his head. "I can't believe you still remember that crazy story about Shatner's gold. You need to forget we ever said there might be gold out there."

My mother grabbed my hand and turned my head so she could look into my eyes. "Josie, darling, we don't really believe there's any gold out there."

I nodded my head, but Mom could see I wasn't convinced.

~

After several more years of preparation, in 1873, with better types of equipment available, my father began to dig the 'Big Ditch' from the north shore of the lake. When it was finished, a deep channel connected Willow Lake to the Kankakee River, a distance of four-and-one-half miles. A restraining dam was built to hold back the water, but now that the ditch was ready, the dam could be opened. Dad announced to the newspaper, the opening of the ditch for Aug. 29, 1874. With the opening of the big ditch, the last vestiges of Willow Lake were anticipated to drain away.

On the appointed day, Dad was as nervous as a hen ready to lay an egg. He paced from the parlor to the kitchen in the spacious entry hall. Stopping, he called up the stairs. "Hurry, Margaret. I want to get to the ditch early. I'm expecting a huge crowd. This is going to be something people around here will talk about for years to come."

I had returned home from school for the spectacle, and Mom and I hurried down the wide stairs dressed in our Sunday best. Our wide skirts swayed and swished with each step down. Hat pins secured our large, feathered hats.

The lowly cabin had long since been replaced by a large two-story frame house displaying the accomplished wealth of my family. Dad had insisted on wide oak trim throughout the house, and oak treads and balusters made the massive stairs the focal point in the large foyer. The rich green stair runner matched the dark green, gold flecked wallpaper throughout the foyer. Stepping down from the final step, I rushed to embrace my father, my long skirt swaying from the quick movement.

"Dad, when can we look for the gold? I want to saddle up Pinto and take a ride to the island."

"The land isn't going to dry that quick I'm afraid. You're not going to be able to ride across the lakebed for months. You need to get this foolishness out of your head. How many times do we need to tell you? There's no gold out there."

I rolled my eyes toward my mother. She laughed, but didn't comment.

Isom waited outside the front of the house with the buggy ready for us to travel to the worksite. I ran to hug him. "So glad to see you again, Miss Josie. Beautiful day for this event."

The day was indeed perfect. The sounds of the geese landing on Willow Lake honking a welcome to more of their kind and an occasional Turtle Dove calling to its mate added to the sound of the clicking of the buggy as the horse's hooves beat against the hardened path. As Dad pulled the horses up toward the mouth of the ditch, he drove past hundreds of interested spectators lined up along the banks on either side. Enjoying the notoriety, he waved to acknowledge all, as he and our small family drove by in our fancy new buggy.

After parking where Mom and I could watch unobstructed, Dad dismounted and walked to the men in charge of the temporary dam. For me, time slowed to a crawl as the men discussed last minute adjustments that I couldn't hear.

"What's taking so long?" I stood to see better. My father looked to be giving final instructions, waving his hands as he spoke, then moved back and faced the men. "Oh, I think they're getting ready to open it. I'm going to walk closer. Want to come?"

"No, you go, dear. I'm not up to walking today." Mom rubbed her brow and flicked her gloved hand motioning for me to go ahead.

Wisps of hair escaped from under my hat and blew around my face from the strong October breeze. The unusually warm day with crystal clear skies almost made it seem like late summer. Most of the men had shed their jackets and the women clutched umbrellas to keep the sun from their faces.

Just as I reached the dam, Dad gave the order, "Okay gentlemen, let's open her up."

Several men pulled back the beams holding back the water. Once the dam was completely opened, a roar came from the onlookers as the greater part of the waters of the big lake rushed down the ditch on their way to the Kankakee River. With the opening of the ditch, a new way of life would become possible with the promise of more land for farm use someday. However, some proclaimed how sad it was that before long most of the fishing and hunting grounds of several generations would be wiped off the map. I myself thought only of the expansion my father planned for the area.

After an hour, most of the onlookers wandered back to their horses or carriages to return home. Dad stayed long enough to be sure the channel had worked properly, then drove us back to Riley's Grove.

"I'm going back to settle up with the workers," said Dad when he drove the buggy around the half circle drive to the front of our house. Dad bounced down to give Mom a hand getting down from the buggy.

Just then Isom pulled up behind us on his horse along with a young cowhand I had never seen before. The young man dismounted and hurried to my side. As he gave me his hand to help me dismount, he held it longer than was necessary. His dark blue eyes pierced through my stubborn façade. Until that moment, I had resisted any suitors. But now, my resolve melted what I had previously felt toward young men. This gent's dark jacket covering his broad shoulders and his long dark hair jutting from under his hat gave him the appearance of a mountain man linked with the look of a local pastor. My insides fluttered in a way I hadn't felt before.

"Josie, go on in now and pack your things. We need to get you back to school tomorrow," said Mother when she saw the look that passed between the young cowhand and me.

"I'm Jim McKnight, Ma'am. Isom hired me to help with the roundup. Hope that's okay with you. I sure could use a job and a place to lay my head," Jim walked toward Mother and extended his hand, but kept his eye on me as he did.

With a forced smile, Mom took Jim's offered hand in her gloved one. "Anyone Isom hires is fine with us, but you'll still have to prove yourself around here." Mother's usual acceptance of outsiders evidently did not extend to a good-looking potential suitor like Jim

McKnight.

Hoping to connect with Jim without an audience, I spent enough time in my room packing to let Mom think I was resting. Then I tiptoed down the stairs and out to the barn. The afternoon sun still warmed the fall day just enough to enjoy a ride. After saddling my horse, I walked him through the back door of the barn. There stood Jim, next to the water trough, with his horse, bridle in hand and a big grin crossing his bronzed face.

"Going somewhere?"

"Been couped up at that school for weeks. I need to get out and connect with the outdoors." I wasn't going to let this cowboy intimidate me even though he had caught my interest. Giving his horse the once over, I gave my horse a pat on the neck. "Want to race? Looks like you've got a pretty fast stallion, but my Pinto is fast, too."

Jim mounted and clicked to his horse, but I had already taken off in the direction of Willow Lake's northern shore. When we reached the swampy lake, already showing only puddles where the deeper water had been, we dismounted and walked our horses along the former sandy shoreline.

"Where's this school you're at?"

"Over in Kankakee. It's called St. Mary's, an all-girls school. I like it, okay. I have two good friends who make it fun when we're not in class. Guess you didn't ask all that though, did you?" Jim's presence made me nervous, and I tended to prattle on when that happened.

Tying both horses to a large oak tree with low sloping branches, Jim motioned for me to follow him to a dry sandy area where we could sit. "Wish you could stay another day. They're having some horse races near Laketown. Thought I might enter Tazz. If somebody doesn't cheat and get a head start, I know I can win. He's the fastest horse I've ever had. Would have liked it if you could have come to cheer me on."

Jim removed his hat and ran his hand through his unruly dark hair. He gave me a sly smile, leaning in closer. I pulled away but smiled back, answering in a soft sultry voice. "Maybe I can convince my dad to stop there on the way back to school."

We sat there on the sand, talking until the sun's light faded and the cool air crept through my light clothing. I shivered and Jim tried to draw me closer, but I got up abruptly. "It's getting late. I need to get back."

Grabbing my reins, I mounted and started for home without waiting for Jim. "Maybe I'll see you tomorrow," I called back to him.

It wasn't difficult to convince my father to stop in Laketown on our way to Kankakee to watch the horse races. Dad never minded putting in a wager every so often, especially if my mother wasn't around.

The horse races ended a day that had been filled with a basket social, speakers and games for young and old. The people of Laketown didn't often get to celebrate but when they did, they made the best of it. Charley Crouse had spent days leveling off a racecourse near the town. The course ran for a quarter mile till the riders turned around a small stand of trees, then back the same quarter mile to the finish line.

Dad parked our buggy facing away from the finish line so our horses wouldn't get any ideas. He tied the reins to a hitching post and was about to help me down, when Jim McKnight rode by, waved and took off at a gallop.

Dad shook his head in dismay. "Is he the reason you wanted to view the races? He's a drifter, Josie. Don't get too close."

I stayed with the team while Dad approached the starting line, where groups of men were gathered collecting bets on the outcome of the race. Shouts rang out above the talk by some who had been drinking more than just lemonade that day. The excitement and noise level rose as the start of the races got closer.

Dad and I found a viewing area not far from the start and finish. It was a good spot to see all the action. The riders were getting ready for the first race, but I hadn't spotted Jim again. Suddenly, a horse and rider came out of the trees just to our left. Jim tipped his hat and as he passed by, he leaned over to hand me his redscarf to wave as he raced.

In the second race, Jim lined up along with the rest of the riders. Holding the horses still was a chore when they knew what the next few minutes had in store for them, but Jim still managed to wave at me. I waved his red scarf as Dad scowled toward Jim. The horses took off like scared rabbits when they heard the gunshot. Jim was in the lead most of the way, but when they rounded the trees, he turned too sharp, and his horse nearly went down. Jim finished third but I still waved his scarf as if he had won.

"Daddy, let's go talk to Jim before we leave for my school."

My father said little as he drove our team toward where Jim was standing, but grumbled under his breath. My stomach turned like a butter churn, anticipating what I would say to Jim. But when we got close, he was so preoccupied with his horse that he hardly noticed us.

"Hopefully, his leg is okay," Jim was saying to one of the other riders, "He's been a good horse for me. Guess I better get him back to the stable and have Doc check him over." As he led Jazz toward the stable, he turned toward us, "Hey, thanks for coming."

We were left standing there like bumps on logs. I looked longingly after Jim still holding the red scarf in my hand. "Well, I'll be. He cares more about that horse than he does about getting to know me."

Dad smiled. "Goes to show, that's the type of treatment you'll get from a cowhand and Jim McKnight is no different."

Chapter 5: 1873

Bailey almost ran into John while reading the open Indianapolis Star. She shoved the paper in front of his eyes. "Look, my first story's been printed. I can't believe it."

Looking over her shoulder, John held Bailey's waist as she read the opening lines of her story. He bent to give her a kiss on her cheek. "Got to go, but I'll be sure and read the whole story later today when I get home. I'm sure it's great."

Bailey folded the paper, so her story was visible and placed it on the table next to the chair by the window where her aunt liked to sit. Then she busied herself cleaning up the breakfast dishes. Hearing Aunt Josie come down the stairs, she held her breath in anticipation. Would her aunt be happy with what she had written? Bailey made a tray with a plate of biscuits with gravy, and a cup of hot coffee to bring to where Aunt Josie was sitting. Her aunt was holding the paper close so she could read the finely printed words.

"What do you think of the first story?"

Aunt Josie laughed. "Kind of boring so far. We've got to get to the interesting parts soon or no one will keep reading."

"Let's get going then," said Bailey.

~

Henry Riley used his huge land holdings first as a range for his large herds of cattle, then as the land was drained, some of the acreage was cultivated to feed the livestock. He became known as the "Prairie King" because of his shrewd dealings in carving out the marshes and prairies of northern Illinois and Indiana. He continued to drain and buy and sell land throughout his lifetime in order to finance his ambitious plans, ultimately becoming one of the richest men in the region.

Each spring driving the cattle to Willow Lake for branding

required all the help my parents could get. The estate buzzed with activity and extra help was needed to feed the cowboys, too. A chuck wagon followed the trek from Illinois across Sugar Island Ford of the Iroquois River eastward into Indiana.

Usually, the roundup was a family affair, but one fall, Mom's poor health kept her from going along on the cattle drive. Standing at their bedroom door, Dad hugged her to say good-bye. He moved halfway down the stairs and turned. "I hate it that we can't ride together this year. I've always enjoyed having you by my side." Seeing Mom's sad face, he hurried back up the steps to give her one more hug. "You rest and be well when I come home."

Mother had always ridden along on the drives, exchanging her dress for men's breeches. But that year she didn't feel up to the grueling ride and the cold night temperatures. She stayed at home and followed a quiet routine of baking, taking slow walks to see what was left of Willow Lake or sitting and working on her needlework.

The drives took almost three days, allowing ample time for grazing time in the evening, which was my father's standard practice of good herd management.

An equal amount of time was necessary for the return to Illinois in the spring. Once arriving back in Illinois, the scene was full of uncommon smells and sounds. The sizzle of red-hot branding irons, the stink of burning hair, and the incessant bawling of wild-eyed cows filled the cool spring air. Dust flew everywhere and the men alternately cursed and filled the air with laughter.

Much to my disappointment, I also missed the drives the two years while at St. Mary's School for girls. During my senior year, the night before the drive was set to begin, Dad visited me at the school.

"Where's Momma?" I called when I met my father in the dormitory foyer. The old building shone with the spit and polish of our required cleaning duties. The plush carpet had been brushed and the old oak furniture dusted and oiled. Dad and Mom had felt St. Mary's was a good choice for my continued education because of the well-rounded curriculum, including domestic training, which meant all the girls were expected to work at cleaning or cooking. To me it seemed the school just managed to get free help, but I didn't complain. I tried to accomplish any assignment the nuns gave me with a pleasant attitude.

"I'm afraid your mother isn't feeling well right now. We both decided it was best that she skipped this year's fall roundup. I'm sure she'll be fine when you get home for the Christmas holiday."

After a light dinner in the refectory with Dad, he left to join the other men waiting to begin the drive in the morning. I retired to my room, but I couldn't get to sleep. Visions of the drive kept whirling around in my head and I longed to be in the midst of the action. Knocking on the doors of my two best friends' rooms, I whispered for them to come across the hall to my room. The girls tiptoed, trying for no sound on the bare wood floor, wearing only their nightgowns and hoping Sister Jean didn't catch us after the curfew. Once inside my room we snuggled together on my small bed.

I flopped onto my side to see my sidekicks better. "I can't get to sleep. I keep thinking about what I'm missing at home."

"We know what and who you're missing," chimed in Patsy, her long blond hair tumbling forward as she spoke. "It's that cowboy you told us about."

"You're not just missing the roundup." Beth laughed and poked me in the side. Beth always had a smile on her lips. She had become my go to when feeling blue.

"I should never have told you two about Jim. I am anxious to see him again, but the roundup is something I hate to miss, and I'm worried about my mom. She isn't well enough to stand the constant movement and excitement of the drive this year." Sighing, I laid my head on Beth's shoulder, then went on. "I love the feeling of freedom the drive gives me. You have to be on your guard all the time and keep the momentum going or you get left behind." I giggled and looked up sheepishly. "But I do wish I could see Jim again, too."

"I knew it. Do you think he'll still be there when you go home for Christmas?" asked Patsy.

I shrugged, not knowing the answer. We talked a little more about things going on at school, then quiet settled in. Each in our own thoughts, we fell off to sleep. Early the next morning Patsy and Beth crept back to their own rooms.

~

Christmas break was a flurry of activity and though I caught glimpses of Jim, my parents kept me tied to the house to help with the holiday preparations. Mom seemed as if she needed more help as time moved on. So, before I knew it, I was back at St. Mary's.

In early June, my parents made a trip to Kankakee to pick me up for my summer break. Following the ridges, at times it took them close to the great slow Kankakee River. When they arrived, my mother described their drive to the school. She painted a word picture of water lilies covering the edges of the slow-moving water and marsh hollyhocks, Dutchmen's Breeches and violets adding color to this pallet.

"Soon the lovely green foliage of May Apples and Jack-In-The-Pulpits will provide a blanket of green. I love feeling the spring breeze rustling through the different trees just beginning to bud. Being close to the river is my favorite part of the trip. It's so beautiful in the spring. We must go back that way to pick black berries and wild strawberries this summer," exclaimed Mom.

Dad nodded but his face showed deep concern. Mom had been able to do less and less, and I feared there would be very few outings in the future.

Dad stabled the horse and wagon at the livery stable near the school. They would stay overnight in one of the rooms set aside for parents when visiting. We planned to leave early the next morning after a quick breakfast.

That evening we enjoyed dinner in the large rectory. Exquisite mahogany dining tables adorned with fine linen were set with a multitude of silverware, ornate crystal glassware and delicate porcelain plates. Sparkling chandeliers cast a warm glow on the luxurious velvet drapes and heavy brocade wallpaper.

After classmates who chose dining room chores served us, I asked, "Have all the hands stayed on after the spring roundup? You probably still needed several to keep up the work." My hopeful expression gave way when neither of my parents answered right away and I caught the glance they shared.

Dad put his hand on mine. "If you're wondering about Jim McKnight, he and several other hired hands moved on to work elsewhere when this last roundup was finished. We just couldn't afford to keep them all on."

I ate in near silence; afraid my disappointment would show in my voice, only answering in short replies to my parents' questions. I hadn't admitted to myself how much I looked forward to seeing

Jim again, and my disappointment felt real.

The next morning, we packed up my belongings and set out for home, moving slowly through the rough roads because of the spring flooding, mainly following the ridge roads. After driving through Momence, the road made a wide path away from the swollen river. The limestone shelf at this point in the river, became a natural dam holding back the flow of the water. The river backed up and spread over the whole area, especially after the spring rains.

Not long after leaving St. Mary's, Mom had fallen asleep with her head resting on my father's shoulder. He wrapped his arm around her as he pulled the buggy to a stop. Pointing to the dammed water, he said, "See the problem there, Josie? Someone needs to break apart that shelf, so the water won't back up and cause flooding. If this can be corrected, our land around Willow Lake could be completely drained and useful.

As we continued further on our trip, Dad became very quiet. I didn't know if he was pondering how he could open up the river or if he was worried about Mother.

The silence suited me fine. I wasn't in the mood for small talk. Finding out Jim had moved on, had upset my plans for the summer. After pulling into the circular drive and stopping in front of the house, I jumped down and ran to my room, leaving Dad to deal with Mother, and Isom to carry my trunks and other bags upstairs.

The summer weeks dragged on with Mom's health diminishing and me moping around the house. Dad couldn't deal with either, so he threw himself deeper into his business dealings, often making overnight trips to Laketown, Momence, or Kankakee. Discussions continued as to how the wide river could be tamed and meetings resulted between the landowners bordering the river in Indiana and Illinois. My father led the charge saying the river needed dredging and the limestone shelf in Momence should be blasted out.

Many afternoons while Mom slept, I rode to Willow Lake with my little shovel tied to my saddle just in case I might see a promising spot that looked like it might hold treasure. I had never given up believing in the story of Shatner's gold. If I could find it, I would be able to buy my own land to work and not have to go back to school in the fall. As much as I enjoyed my friends, I wanted to move on and be treated like an adult.

On the rise that had once been Refuge Island, I dug several holes. As I started on the fourth, a rustling behind me caught my attention, then a horse's whinny made me turn. I raised the shovel above my head in defense, but the horse and rider were hidden behind the brush. Someone yelled, "What in the world are you doing?"

That voice. I recognized it and smiled. "Jim McKnight, what are you doing spying on me?"

Jim rode out from behind the brush. He dismounted and walked toward me. "Had to come back and see if you missed me just a little."

Keeping the shovel between us, I stood my ground. Jim moved closer, ignoring the shovel. His hands grabbed for my waist, and he pulled me close. Dropping the shovel, I raised my head, and our kiss set off something inside me that I'd never felt before. I tried to step back but Jim held me tighter and kissed me again. He took a step back and held me at arm's length for a few more seconds, staring into my eyes.

"Man, you've got into my head, girl. I can't seem to think about anything else."

I smiled, trying to act innocent, then looked intently toward the ground. "I've got to get back home, but meet me tonight in the barn hayloft. I'll bring something to eat, and we can have a picnic."

Jim hurried back to his horse and called back, "It'll be too dark for a picnic, but we'll think of something to keep us occupied."

I watched as Jim rode away. The rest of my summer was about to become much more interesting.

~

Bailey looked up from her writing pad. Aunt Josie had fallen asleep right when things were really getting interesting. She might have to wait until tomorrow to write more about her aunt's notorious life. Reading over what she had just written, it seemed the next newspaper story would definitely be more interesting. Using the notes she had taken so far; she started to write the beginning of the article.

Chapter 6

Aunt Josie woke with a start, her head bobbing against the back of the wing-back chair. "Oh dear, Bailey, you should have woken me."

"It's fine. I took the last few minutes to reorganize my notes. We can work again tomorrow, but I'm anxious to find out what happened with you and Jim."

Aunt Josie's cheeks turned a rosy color. "I need to freshen up, but if you still have some time, I can go on with my story."

1873

All summer Jim and I met clandestinely whenever we could. Meeting in the loft at night, or during the day, out by Refuge Island, we couldn't keep our emotions under control, if you know what I mean. When Mother asked what I was doing out at Willow Lake all the time, I used the excuse that I was still looking for the buried treasure, which wasn't a lie. I continued the search somewhat. After confiding to Jim about the Shatner gold, he was more than willing to help me dig in many more locations.

"Are you sure there's gold here? I'm tired of digging these holes. Let's take a little break." Jim waggled his eyebrows letting me know what he meant.

"Oh, all right, but we're not done looking. It's got to be here somewhere."

Because of my relationship with Jim, I had become a pleasant person to be around for the rest of that summer. My parents soon noticed the change in my disposition. I smiled and hummed as I did the chores around Riley's Grove, even asking how I could help out occasionally. But toward the middle of August, things changed. I was so tired and every morning I felt nauseous. I begged to stay in bed most mornings and when I did get up, Mother could hear me retching in the chamber pot.

She stormed into my room not long after one such incident. "You've been sneaking off with that cowhand, Jim McKnight, haven't you?"

I ran to Mom's side and sobbed on her shoulder. "What am I going to do? Can you have Daddy talk to Jim for me?"

My father pounded on my door that evening and didn't wait for me to call for him to come in. "I told you to stay away from that cowboy. Now, look at yourself."

Tears streamed down my face and Dad's face softened. "Daddy, what am I going to do? I love him, but I don't think he wants to get married." My shoulders shook with another round of blubbering.

Dad's face became hard again, but his eyes glistened. My father folded me in his embrace. "I'll be talking to that young man, don't you worry."

When Dad found Jim the next day, he made it clear there would be a wedding soon. "I expect you to ask for Josie's hand in marriage. The sooner the better. You'll work for me again. We can't have our daughter following you around from ranch to ranch."

My parents reluctantly agreed to accept Jim into our family circle. Jim could now come to the Riley homestead, and he and I no longer had to hide our relationship. But something seemed to have cooled in Jim's attention toward me. When we sat together on the swing hanging from the ceiling of the wide front porch, he barely looked at me.

"What's the matter? I thought you loved me."

Jim twirled his wide brimmed hat in his hands. "It's just that I never planned on taking on a wife and now a kid. I kind of liked moving on from time to time."

When I heard those words, in my fragile condition, tears began to stream down my face. Jim couldn't stand to see me cry either, so he took me in his arms. "It'll be okay, Josie. Don't cry. I'll try to be a good husband and father."

He must have some feelings for me, but he'd have to do better than that. "Try?" I hit him square in the belly, and he doubled over. "You'll have to do better than try."

Jim sputtered out a breathless reply, "Okay, I promise I'll stick around for you and the baby."

His promise meant I had the upper hand when it came to dealing with our future, at least for a while. My parents made the best of the situation and planned a beautiful wedding, inviting their friends and all the notable landowners near Riley's Grove. Guests came from as far away as Kankakee. Extra beds were made up in the house and barn to accommodate overnight guests.

On the day of the wedding, my father played the organ as I walked to meet Jim, dressed in the white dress Mom had worn for her wedding. Jim fidgeted at the front of the barn, looking as if he wanted to run away like a jack rabbit being chased by a coyote. He looked so handsome dressed in his black coat, white shirt and borrowed tie; my fears disappeared for the time it took to enjoy the party.

Mom ordered oysters from Momence and Isom cooked pheasants accompanied by a special sauce he made. The dishes were served buffet style. Two long tables lined the edges of the main room of the barn, filled with platters of cold game, trays of oysters on ice, an assortment of bread and rolls, pickles and a variety of cheeses. Mrs. Jaynes made a beautifully decorated cake for dessert.

Dancing and merriment continued until well after midnight, with Jim and me leading the group in dances like the quadrille and Waltz. The jovial evening later proved to be the high point of my relationship with Jim. In the months that followed, he began working long days on the homestead, while I spent many hours alone in my parents' former cabin, where Jim and I now lived. Trying to make the best of things, I spent much of my time sewing clothes and knitting blankets for the baby.

As fall turned into winter Mom often needed help because of her failing health, and I made it a point to take the short walk to their home about every day. I did my best to decorate and bake as much as Mother had always done for Christmas, but with Mom in bed much of the day, the joy of the season dwindled, along with the love I had felt for Jim.

"Where's my dinner? I expect some food after working all day," Jim yelled, coming in late again with booze on his breath. He staggered in and collapsed onto the chair by the hearth.

"It was ready," I yelled back, "but I threw it to the hog. Where were you, again?"

"Been doing some more digging," he slurred. "Got to be out there somewhere."

"You didn't let anyone see you, did you? That's my gold."

"Don't worry. Ole Jim knows how to keep a secret. Come here and let me feel that little feller inside your belly."

I moved closer, but kept just enough distance so Jim couldn't grab me to sit on his lap. Jim's hand caressed my stomach. "Got to get some money so we can move on, away from your parents."

I just let him talk. He would never have the money to move, and I would not go with Jim even if he

found a way. My mother needed me right now and I needed Mom for the birth of my child. If Jim wanted to leave, then fine. At least our child wouldn't have to hear our constant fighting.

Our lovemaking had been so much fun, but now after real life barged in, I found I was ill-equipped to deal with this marriage to such an unruly cow hand. Why hadn't I seen it sooner? Jim's looks had turned my head, but I hadn't looked into his soul. We had very little in common and I dreaded spending the rest of my life with this man. In my next letters to Patsy and Beth, I would warn them and suggest they make better choices when looking for partners than I had.

When the snow had almost melted and patches of green began to show through the dirty white drifts, I woke to cool air inside the cabin. Jim had let the fire die out again. The March winds sang through some of the unchinked cracks, and I would have turned over under the quilts, but the pains I felt warned me it must be time.

"Jim, go get my mother and Mrs. Jaynes. The baby's coming." I heard nothing. Where was he? Again, I yelled. This time Jim came stomping into the cabin with a load of wood in his arms.

"Had to use the privy and get wood. What's going on?"

Once I made the urgency clear to my husband, he ran out of the cabin without asking if I needed anything. I tried to get up, but water gushed out of me, soaking the bed. Laying there in the wet bed, I decided again this was not what I had bargained for when having fun with Jim last summer. Why had I lost my head over a cowhand? I made up my mind that day. In the future, I would not be dependent on any man.

Once baby Crawford joined us, Jim settled into the job of father much better than I had expected. Often on Sunday afternoons when Jim was off work, he would hitch up the wagon and take our little family out for a picnic to the nearly dry Willow Lake. The initial draining of the lake had left pockets of marshland where stagnant water filled small depressions, and only during very dry seasons was the lakebed usable for pasture. Dad often talked about ways to make the property functional, but so far nothing more had been done.

After spreading out a blanket and sitting with me for a light lunch, Jim held Crawford while I packed up the lunch and did some necessary business behind a tree. Walking back, I couldn't help but notice how Crawford's hair matched Jim's dark locks rather than my auburn ones.

When I returned, he said, "Here, take him. I think he soiled himself. I'm going to go dig in a couple more spots That gold has to be here somewhere."

"I wish I had never told you the story about Shatner's gold. You're more obsessed than I ever was."

But holding Crawford close, I soon joined in the hunt for more places to dig, only to be disappointed again and again. When the afternoon sun dipped below the tree line, we packed up and trotted our horse and buggy back to the cabin in frustration. Jim's sullen disposition became worse each time his future looked bleaker, often taking it out on me with verbal abuse. So far, he had not tried anything physical, and since Dad was Jim's employer, in a way, I still had the upper hand.

When Crawford turned two and was able to stay with his grandparents for a couple days, Jim convinced me to travel to Kankakee with him to visit an old friend. I looked forward to the trip just to get away for a short time.

Riding along in the warm spring weather, I pulled off my bonnet to let my auburn curls catch the breeze. Letting my hair blow gave me a feeling of freedom I hadn't experienced since before Crawford was born. I felt closer to Jim than I had for a long time, and our evening spent in the hotel in Kankakee rekindled some of the love I had once felt for the man.

The next morning Jim let me sleep and left early to meet with his friend. Later, hearing loud voices outside in the hallway, I knew Jim had been drinking. He burst through the door followed by another gentleman who was more refined than Jim ever could be.

His piercing green eyes stared straight into mine from atop his tall lanky frame. The two men appeared to hail from distinctly different backgrounds. The immaculate attire and posture of Jim's companion stood in stark contrast to Jim's somewhat disheveled appearance at that moment.

"Meet my new partner, Josie, Harry Feldman," slurred Jim. "We're going to open a saloon right here in Kankakee. No more working for your father

Chapter 7:

1874-1879

I did not move to Kankakee with Jim. I couldn't. Not with the way Mother was feeling most days. Crawford and I moved back into my parents' home and Jim came back occasionally to see us. This arrangement worked well for a while. However, his talk about the saloon and how great it was doing made me a little jealous. Why couldn't he be satisfied to stay here with us?

"Every night the saloon is full of paying customers and the show the dance girls put on is fabulous. Harry and I are making tons of money. We'll be able to pay off our loan in no time," Jim bragged.

Dad shook his head. "Maybe you could hand over some of that cash to support your wife and son."

Jim laughed. "Won't be long and I'll be able to send loads of money this way and maybe even buy some land for us to have our own home built."

I never took much stock in Jim's boasting. He always left after a few days, and I had yet to see any help in the way of cash.

Life on the homestead fell into a rhythm with me taking over most of the household chores. I helped the servant girl wash clothes in a kettle over an open fire, made lye soap in that same kettle, put bread out to rise, and sewed and mended clothes for myself and Crawford. Tending the garden and my beloved flowers and pruning the fruit trees filled my warm spring days.

Once Crawford turned four, on one of Jim's rare visits, he began teaching Crawford to ride by walking him around the corral on the smallest and oldest horse available. Crawford's large blue eyes grew wider each time they circled around near me as I hung on the fence watching. A large stand of oaks framed the small corral on the west side making Crawford and the pony look tiny in comparison. I watched with growing trepidation as Jim started guiding the horse faster each time around.

"He's going to fall and break his head open," I called out. Secretly, I hoped Jim would continue to feel a connection with

Crawford. Maybe then he would want to stay on the homestead and help with the raising of our son.

But Jim never again felt an attachment to the hard work of a homestead. He loved the atmosphere of his saloon, the free and easy talk, the card games and the liquor that never ran out. I found it difficult to understand why he could not be satisfied with the commitment of living on the farm. I began to see that Jim and I were obviously unsuited to be married to one another. We were both too dominating to live peaceably together. Jim needed a pliant, docile woman who would unquestionably follow whatever path he chose to take. I was not that woman. I began plotting how I could get a divorce.

Keeping these thoughts to myself proved difficult, but because of Crawford, I didn't let anyone know how I felt. He loved it when Jim visited, and Jim doted on Crawford while at the homestead. For our son's sake, I put my own feelings aside and often begged, "Couldn't you stay longer? Crawford really misses you when you go."

He always had some excuses. "Sorry, got to make it back to go over the books with Harry. Got to keep an eye on him or he'll steal me blind." Jim laughed but I wondered if this might be true.

"Not a great partner to have then, if you ask me."

Ignoring my comment, he hugged Crawford, gave me a kiss on the cheek, and continued his preparations to leave.

There must have been some flaw in Jim's character that made him seek the saloon life rather than spending quiet evenings reading aloud to his family like my father had done when I was a young girl and what he often did now with Crawford. It was just beyond my understanding why he didn't want to spend all his time near his son. To his credit he gave up asking me to join him in the city. He knew I would never leave Mother in her condition.

On one evening when Jim visited, we sat in front of the fire just like the married couple I wanted us to be. Jim became so excited telling me about the raucous life of the saloon that I almost wished I could go and see what it was like for myself. "We have all sorts of clientele. That's what makes running the saloon so interesting. Solid citizens mingle with illegal scum, and no one asks questions. We keep a gun handy under the bar, just in case of trouble but so far, we haven't had to use it. We're making good money, now, too."

I must admit the money was appreciated. Jim had been bringing cash whenever he came to the homestead. I kept squirreling it away for a day when I'd need to be on my own and that day came sooner than we all expected.

In the spring of 1879, I woke up on a Monday morning to a curiously quiet house. Running to my mother's room, I checked to see if she was all right. I tiptoed to her bedside and noticed the same shallow breathing she always exhibited lately. Her dark hair sprawled around her pale features like an open fan, making her look like a sweet angel who had come to earth.

Leaving her so she could get much needed sleep, I hurried to Crawford's room, which he shared with Jim when he visited. When I opened the door, the silence hit me like an empty tomb. Neither of my guys were in bed. Looking out the window, I saw that Jim's horse was no longer in the corral.

I went into the room where Dad had started sleeping so he wouldn't disturb Mother's rest. "Dad," I loud whispered so as not to wake mother in the room next door. "Dad, I think Jim took Crawford."

Rubbing his eyes, Dad sat up and flipped his legs to the side of the bed. "What? Are you sure?"

Dad dressed as quickly as possible, and I returned to my room to do the same. After taking a quick look around the homestead, Dad asked Isom to hitch up the wagon. After checking with the housekeeper to stay and take care of Mother, we threw in a few supplies, and Dad and I rushed to make a trip to Kankakee.

The spring rains had made deep ruts in the roadway and several times Dad and I had to get out and place dead branches under the wagon wheels to get through the mud. The horses struggled to walk, making a sucking noise each time they lifted their hooves from the mud. Hours later, we pulled up in front of Jim's saloon late in the afternoon. I ran into the place while Dad attended to the horses.

Breaking through the door, I yelled, "Where's Jim McKnight?" Everyone turned to look at me, but most went back to their activity of drinking or playing cards or both. I recognized Harry standing behind the bar and moved to question him. "Where's Jim?"

He nodded to the stairway, so I took the flight by twos, not sure which room was Jim's, but then I heard my son's laugh followed by a woman's cackle. I pounded on the door, and Jim's voice called out, "It's open."

I burst in and found one of the dancehall girls on Jim's lap and little Crawford on top of hers. My head nearly exploded from all the anger inside it. Grabbing Crawford in my arms, I rushed for the door. All I could think of was getting him out of that place. Taking the stairs even faster than when I went up, I carried him to the door just as Dad entered and I handed him over to my father. We both turned to see Jim on the upper landing. "Get Crawford out of here, Dad. Take him to the buckboard and be ready to leave."

Jim pulled a pistol out of his waistcoat and aimed it toward me. He called out in a slurring voice. "Josie, he wants to be with his dad. Don't you dare take him out of here."

When the patrons saw the gun, they scattered, and most left the saloon by the back door. Harry and the rest of the customers ran out the front. After a couple more seconds, the girl that had been on Jim's lap came up behind him on the landing, her dress showing an overabundance of cleavage. Jim must have thought it was someone who wanted to subdue him because he turned abruptly and his gun went off, shooting her right in the foot. She howled like a banshee and began dancing around on her other foot. I saw my chance, remembering Jim had said they had kept a gun behind the bar. While the two on the landing were distracted, I moved there to grab that gun and hiding behind the bar ready for Jim to come down.

Jim yelled at the bawling girl, "Keep quiet. I can't think." Then to me he said, "Josie, I'm not giving up my kid. If I have to kill you, I will."

The girl continued making such a racket and I could see Jim's nerves were unraveling. Feeling like I needed to do something, I stood and took a shot toward the ceiling above the landing. Becoming disoriented, Jim shot off several rounds hitting bottles behind the bar and several wooden tables and chairs. I didn't want either of us to get hurt and leave Crawford with only one parent or neither, but I couldn't let Jim harm me or the innocent girl, so I shot again in the vicinity of the landing.

This time the bullet ricocheted off the metal hinge of the closest door and hit Jim in his shin. When he grabbed where the bullet nicked him, he leaned back too far into the railing. At that point everything started happening faster than a greased pig race. The railing broke loose, and Jim tumbled off the landing down to the large slabs of black walnut flooring at the lower level of the saloon. I ran to him to see if I could help but I saw the odd angle of his head and neck and knew he was gone.

"Someone call the sheriff," I called out. My mind went out to my son. How would I ever explain this to Crawford?

When everyone came back in to see the outcome of our shootout and the sheriff arrived to question the witnesses, everyone agreed it was obvious that Jim's death was the result of the fall. However, as time went on, the rumors continued that I had shot and killed my own husband. I never did live that down.

~

"Now, that was not boring. This will make a great publication," said Bailey.

Aunt Josie straightened her skirt and laughed a little. "Looking back, when I see that poor girl dancing around up on that landing holding her foot, I can't help but chuckle to myself. It really is such a funny and bittersweet tale. Having Jim out of the picture made for an easier life for me to raise Crawford how I saw fit, but I missed him after that. In his own way, he wasn't a bad person, he was probably a Scotchman, that's all."

Bailey laughed. "What's that got to do with anything? I don't think I'll write that in my next story, but the rumors that you killed your husband will be stopped as soon as I can write this up and it's printed in the Star."

Josie's face went dark. "You know, I could be changing these stories to suit my reputation." While dabbing at her eyes and pushing back a strand of loose hair, Josie gave Bailey a slow, wry smile.

Bailey opened her mouth to speak, but the words caught in her throat. Her eyes opened as wide as silver dollars. Was Aunt Josie using her as her pawn?

A wide smile formed across her aunt's face. "Your face was priceless, dear. Don't worry. My stories are mostly true."

Chapter 8:

1879-1883

Jim had no other family as far as we knew, so we buried him in the family plot near Willow Lake. Years before, Dad had fenced off a small parcel and put up a marker for the baby my parents had buried somewhere near Indianapolis on the trail to the homestead. Jim's grave gave the small space the feeling of permanence, as if an actual body made it a real graveyard. We didn't know it at the time, but it wasn't long after Jim was laid to rest that another grave site would soon be added to the small plot.

Mother insisted on joining the procession to the gravesite for Jim's funeral, but with the continuing spring rains threatening again, my father made an extra cover for the buggy so she wouldn't get wet. However, just being out in the damp, cold weather seemed to take a toll on her. For the next few days after the funeral, Mom spent most of the time in her bed, only sitting up when either Dad or I would bring her a meal. The large four-poster bed nearly swallowed her small frame. Failing more each day, she reminded me of a porcelain doll that we couldn't play with for fear of breaking.

Dad warned me, his voice faltering. "We need to prepare ourselves for the worst, Josie."

Immediately, I knew what he meant, but I didn't want to face the facts. What would I do without my mother's strong influence on my life? She was my rock and confidant, my best friend. She had taught me to be the strong woman I had become and encouraged me even when I let her down. Mom had such strength of character, generosity and good humor that all who knew her, loved her, but that spirit seemed to be ebbing away.

Once the worst of the cold, wet spring weather passed and the promise of warmer weather was on the horizon, Mom rallied somewhat. On Crawford's birthday in late March, she dressed in one of her beautiful gowns and came down for the celebration. The dress hung loosely on her small frame, but we were all happy she was making the effort to join in. I had baked a cake and invited Isom and a couple of the servants to join us. Six candles adorned the cake and Dad and Isom made ice cream to top off the celebration.

"Let's see if you can blow out all the candles at once," said Isom after carrying Crawford on piggyback to the chair at the head of the table. My little man was growing up so fast. And as he grew older, the resemblance to Jim became uncanny, a constant reminder of my flawed choice. But having Crawford proved good could be the result, even when choosing badly,

"I want Grandmama to help." Crawford waved to Mother to sit next to him, so she ceremoniously took Dad's arm as he helped her to the table.

When everyone had gathered around the dining room table, I lit the candles. We huddled around the cake and Dad called out, "Okay, on three. One, two, three." Mom's feeble attempt made little difference in the movement of the air, but Crawford made up for her lack of wind. Dad placed his hand on Mother's shoulder, supporting her as he always had.

After that brief interlude, Mother's health seemed to deteriorate even faster. Dad fetched a doctor from Momence, but Dr. Eggert just shook his head. "Make her comfortable and keep her sitting up as much as possible to keep the pneumonia at bay."

Most days, Dad would lift Mom into the chair near the upstairs window. Looking out at the green pastures and forests below, she spoke amid winded breaths. "We chose well when we picked this spot for our homestead, Henry. It has been a wonderful home."

Dad's eyes shone with unshed tears as he held her hand and nodded his agreement.

Gradually, even the hour sitting in the chair became too much for Mom. She began retaining so much fluid that her body looked half again larger. She was no longer conscious of us who stood by her side for her last few days. Dad and I, Crawford and even Isom were by her bedside when she slipped away. Our lives were full of sadness and loss, but she was no longer suffering. We laid her to rest alongside the baby's marker. Perhaps now they could be reunited.

After several months of intense grief, my father threw himself back into the work of the homestead, handling the cattle and horse business just as he and mother had done together. Feeling relieved that he had made the decision to move on, I was tasked with cleaning out mother's room and dealing with her personal items. I kept almost everything except the items she wore while the sickness advanced and took over her body.

For a year after Mom's death, Dad ate poorly and spent too much time working. As a result, his appearance and demeaner changed. His clothes hung on his once robust frame and his coloring changed from rosy cheeks to pale. His happy disposition became brooding and even Crawford couldn't get him to smile at dinner.

"Grandpa, I rode my horse all on my own today. I even helped saddle him."

Dad barely looked up. "That's good to hear."

This dismal existence became unbearable for me. I needed to move on. With both Jim and my mother gone, and Crawford at the age where he wasn't benefiting from my teaching him at home, I made the decision to move so he could go to school. I decided to use the money Jim had left me for a house in Momence where I could take in boarders and where Crawford could attend school.

This idea did not sit well with my father. When I told him my plan, he replied in anger, "No, I won't hear of it. I need you here."

One morning Dad came home after an overnight trip to Kankakee and slapped a paper down in front of me on the table where I sat teaching Crawford some figures.

"What's this?"

"It's a gift, well almost. Legally you owe me one dollar. I'm hoping it will entice you to stay, Josie."

Picking up the paper, at the top I noticed a legal heading, 'Warranty Deed.' After skimming the first few paragraphs, my head pounded with excitement. "You're giving me the land under Willow Lake? Four thousand forty acres of lakebed?"

"Yes, now you can look for gold all you want, and there'll be no question whose it is, if you find it."

"What gold?" asked Crawford with eyes as big as the gold pieces I had always imagined.

"Never mind, your grandpa is just being silly and a little crazy." I stood to give my father a hug, something I hadn't done much of since Mother passed. Not to be outdone, Crawford joined us in the family union. Dad started laughing, the first I'd heard from him since Mother died.

I let the gesture go unheeded for several days and then confronted my father. "Dad, I'm sorry, but the property doesn't change the fact that I need to get Crawford in school and the best way for me to do that is to move to Momence. I've already put money down on a house and I can't back out now. But don't worry, we'll be sure to visit Riley's Grove whenever we can."

Dad's face sank, his sad eyes made me want to change my mind. My insides churned like a runaway rabbit, but I needed to stay strong. If I stayed, Dad would try to take over every detail of my life and we'd end up hating one another.

Isom helped me pack up our personal belongings onto the wagon, along with some of the furniture from the cabin Jim and I had lived in when first married. Looking like a rockslide ready to topple, the load must have reminded my father of the move he and mother made from Ohio. My heart felt broken in two when on the morning of our move, Dad was nowhere to be seen.

Isom climbed up onto the wagon seat next to Crawford and me. "He'll come around, Josie. Don't worry about your dad. He'll be so busy with those cattle that he won't be able to think of anything else."

The large house that I purchased in Momence had been built by a well-known banker. It had four rooms upstairs that could be rented to boarders and a large bedroom on the main floor for Crawford and me. A separate dining room, and a formal living room, could be used by all my prospective renters and the large kitchen would be perfect for making meals for my boarders.

I hung my sign out as soon as Isom got us settled and before long I had several inquiries regarding renting rooms. Two young men who were traveling salesmen rented but would be in and out according to their sales routes. One of Crawford's would-be teachers stopped by and moved in before the term started. Then a young man named John Dreger rented the last available room saying he would only need it for a short time because he was in the process of buying a place close to the DeMotte community. After each rental, I had to purchase additional furniture, which used up more of my savings.

Settling into a normal routine and getting Crawford in school proved to be a great choice, at least for a while. After a couple months, Dreger moved on, and the room stood empty for almost four months. I became a little desperate because I needed to rent all four rooms to keep my finances in the black. Borrowing from my father was not an option if I could help it. In fact, I hadn't heard much from him in the last few months. I found I was too busy to return to Riley's Grove except for the holidays and Dad had quit stopping by on his work trips. I missed him terribly, but I kept telling myself if I didn't hear from him, it meant he was busy and doing okay.

My life changed dramatically one day when a tall, handsome man knocked on the door of my boarding house. His piercing blue eyes crinkled somewhat when he smiled and his short, dark hair fell over his forehead in tiny curls. Dressed in pin stripe trousers, a brown waistcoat and a dark tweed tailcoat, he gave the impression of being a successful businessman. "I'd like to rent your room if it's still available."

I nearly jumped into his arms. I opened the door wider, and I welcomed him into the foyer. "Yes, of course. May I ask your name and what business you're in?"

Watching me closely, his smile faded and his face went quite dark. "My name is Charles Rainey, but I'd rather not state my business."

With that he handed me a month's rent and picked up his valise. I escorted him up the stairs to his room and handed him the key. Little did I know that Charles would become a big part of my life in the next few months.

~

Bailey put down her pencil. "This sounds like it might be getting intriguing again. Does he end up being another love interest?'

"You'll just have to wait until tomorrow. Now go make dinner for your dear husband and let an old lady rest a bit."

Chapter 9

The next morning, when Aunt Josie didn't come down for breakfast, Bailey went up and knocked on her door. "Are you okay, Aunt Josie? We missed you at breakfast."

"I feel a little under the weather so I'm going to rest a bit more. I'm sure I'll be down for lunch."

True to her words, Aunt Josie joined John and Bailey for the noon meal. John sat reading the newspaper and barely spoke until he ran across Bailey's most recent story.

"Guess we have a celebrity in our midst. Bailey is painting quite a picture in words about you, Aunt Josie." He looked toward Bailey and smiled. Josie fluttered her hands as if shewing away flies.

Feeling relieved that John approved, Bailey said, "It's all the God's truth, isn't it, Aunt Josie?"

Josie laughed. "Well, it's the way I remember it. Maybe not the way God saw it. By the way, I'm feeling better so after we get this food cleaned up, come into the parlor and I can continue with my tale. You never know how many days I have left; you know."

Bailey caught John's face light up. Was he anxious to get rid of her or did Aunt Josie's comment amuse him?

1884

My new boarder, Mr. Rainey, proved to be both a mystery and a companionable conversationalist at each meal he attended. Sometimes after being gone for a few days, he returned with stories that he told in an animated voice for the entertainment of all the boarders. When he spun an unusually far-fetched tale, he laughed louder and longer than his audience, while proclaiming its truth. As

I busied myself serving the food and cleaning up, each time I stole a look toward him, his eyes met mine and my insides did a flip-flop.

Then one evening after making sure Crawford did his homework, when I came back to the dining room to do more cleaning, Mr. Rainey still occupied the spot where he had been sitting when eating with the other boarders. A bottle containing a brown liquid and a glass half full sat in front of him. "Come sit with me for a bit."

"I don't make a habit of consorting with my boarders, Mr. Rainey."

His raucous laugh rose to the ceiling and I'm sure the hanging oil light above the table tingled with the waves of sound.

"Consorting, huh? That sounds immoral." He stared at me with that teasing smile of his, and I felt as if he had undressed me at that moment. "How about we just talk? Would that be, okay?"

"I suppose that will be fine." I pulled out the chair opposite him, far enough away so there could be no touching. Sitting with my hands in my lap, I looked everywhere in the room except at Rainy's face. This didn't seem to bother the man. He prattled on about anything and everything, while refilling his glass every so often.

This went on for many nights and eventually I moved to the chair next to Charles. He had requested I call him by his given name when the two of us were alone. Before long, when I was able to find time, and Charles was not on one of his business jaunts, we began spending more time together going for picnics and long rides along the Kankakee.

Charles also took a shine to Crawford and the feeling seemed to be mutual especially when Charles offered to set up a shooting range and help Crawford learn to shoot his rifle. He showed Crawford how to load the shells, how to release the safety, and how to use the lever action each time he wanted to take a shot.

I set up some tin cans on a rock behind the boarding house, about thirty feet away.

"When do I get to shoot?" asked Crawford, his lanky frame reminding me again of Jim.

"Watch me, first, okay?" Charles shot five times and each of the five cans went flying. "Go set them up again and then you can try. I hope you were watching closely."

Crawford ran to set up the cans and returned to take his turn at shooting. He took the gun off safety, pulled the lever and held the gun like he thought he should. He pulled the trigger before asking if he was doing everything correctly.

"Ooww! My shoulder!"

Charles burst out laughing. "I told you to watch me. You've got to rest the gun against your shoulder, so, it won't kick quite so much. Now try it again and get your position right before you shoot. You want to lean forward a little and bend your knees slightly so your body can move with the recoil of the gun."

Charles swayed a little when he again showed Crawford the stance. Walking closer, I smelled the distinct odor of whisky. Charles had been drinking more frequently, but I didn't think he would this early in the day and when he was around Crawford. My rage increased as I let Crawford finish shooting another round of cans. "That's enough for now. Crawford, go and get your chores done."

"Can I shoot again later?"

My voice had risen a pitch. "We'll see. Now go or for sure I won't let you."

Standing with my hands on my hips, my heart felt like a hammer inside my chest. "You're drinking while you're teaching my son to shoot?"

"Oh, hold on, I only had one drink. Besides I thought you liked a party as much as anyone." Charles grabbed for my waist, but I twisted out of his grasp and hurried toward the house.

Flushed from running, I entered the foyer and got the surprise of my life when I found my father standing in the parlor talking with a young woman. They both turned to look my way, and a moment of awkward silence ensued. I caught my breath, wiped my brow with the back of my hand and walked toward them. The woman looked younger than me and sported the newest in fashion. Her tan silk dress consisted of the newest style form-fitting bodice, and she wore no bustle to speak of. With the large puffy sleeves she presented a smart overall appearance. I looked down at my untidy blouse and skirt of heavy fabric wishing I had not run the distance back to the house. Pushing back whisps of hair that had fallen into my face, I tried to compose myself and moved closer to the two of them.

"Dad, I wish you had sent word that you would be visiting. I could have prepared a special meal." I hugged my father and looked toward the girl, waiting for an introduction from my dad.

"We're not planning on staying, Josie." Then with a flourish, as if welcoming a princess, he continued. "But I wanted you to meet my fiancé, Elizabeth May Woodburn. She is the daughter of one of my business acquaintances. We plan to be married at a small ceremony next week in Kankakee. We're on our way there now. We would like you to come, if you please."

I stood in stunned silence. This could not be. My father still loved my mother. He would never get married again. This girl couldn't be more than twenty-five years old. How could he do this to the memory of my mother? Trying to calm myself, I again tried to speak, "Daddy, can I speak with you privately?"

"Whatever you have to say, you need to say it to both of us." Dad then drew Elizabeth close to his side with his extended arm and held the two of them in that pose.

I felt my insides begin to twirl and feeling faint, I sat down in the nearest chair. Just then, Crawford came from our room. "Grandfather, I'm so happy to see you. You haven't visited for so long." Crawford gave Dad one of those side hugs men and boys so often do, now just as tall as his grandfather. After a moment he noticed Elizabeth entangled with his grandfather on the opposite side. "Who is this? She's very pretty."

"I'm glad you think so. I do too, and that's one reason I am going to marry this pretty lady. I hope you will think of her as your grandmother, Crawford."

Crawford's blue eyes became as round as a full moon. "I will do my best, but she does not look like a grandmother."

"Crawford, manners, please." I couldn't think of anything else to say. The clock's ticking became the only sound in the room as Crawford continued to stare at his new grandmother.

Dad's voice broke the silence. "Well, we will be on our way. The wedding is on Friday, a week from today. I would like to have you there, but I understand if you can't get away." Dad ushered Elizabeth toward the door to leave.

At this point Elizabeth had still not said a word, and I began to worry that she might be mute. Crawford and I followed the couple out to their carriage, the very one my father and mother had used when she was alive. Had my father gone completely mad? Loneliness must be an awful thing. I wanted to kick myself for not visiting more often and maybe he wouldn't be in this predicament.

Dad helped Elizabeth into the carriage and as he walked to climb up the other side, she nodded her head and said, "So nice to meet you."

"Yes, likewise." I stammered.

The fury I felt towards my father did not subside by the following week, so I did not go to the wedding. I told myself I couldn't get anyone to run the boarding house in time, but it was just an excuse. Several friends had offered to take over if I wanted to go. Charles suggested he could drive me, but he often wasn't sober enough to make a long drive, so I didn't take him up on his offer, either. The date passed with not another word from the happy couple for several months. Then in December, I received a hand-written invitation from Elizabeth to come for a Christmas get-together at Riley's Grove. For my father's sake, I made plans with Charles and Crawford to attend.

Walking into my family home, I nearly collapsed with sadness. The Yuletide decorations looked so much like what my mother had always done. Had Dad directed Elizabeth to do the same? How would I ever get through this visit?

Elizabeth greeted us, "I'm so happy you decided to come. Henry has been like a schoolboy making sure everything is just so. I hope it makes you feel welcome."

Apparently, Elizabeth had found her tongue. 'This is my home,' I wanted to shout, but just then Isom entered, and I hurried to him for a hug. His white hair topped a more wrinkled face, and his body stooped somewhat but his strong voice made me feel welcome. "So good to see you, Miss Josie."

He helped carry our bags to our upstairs rooms. "Sure, ain't like it was when your mama ran this house. Things are plum crazy around here."

"It's okay, Isom. Guess she makes my father happy." I didn't believe it myself, but I was trying to keep peace for the sake of the season and for my father.

Charles soon knocked on my door with a drink in each hand and I welcomed the spirits to bring an end to my swirling insides.

Chapter 10: 1884-1885

Returning home to the boarding house, I spent the next few days after that awful Christmas doing very little, only what needed attention and cooking and baking the bare necessities. When Charles suggested attending a New Year's Eve party and dance in Kankakee, my first thought was wanting to spend the night with Crawford in front of a fire reading and an early bedtime.

But Charles continued to pester me. "You need to get out and have some fun. You've been moping around ever since we got back from Riley's Grove."

I felt I had a reason to mope. Not only had I lost my husband and my mother, but now, my father expected me to accept his new young wife. How much was I supposed to bear at such a young age? I didn't care to be another Job, who lost all and still insisted on thanking God for all he had. I just wanted to wallow in my misery and yes, blame God for my troubles.

Crawford brought me out of my musings. "Mom, you need to go. I'm going to spend the night at Davie's house, so you'd be all alone."

"Young man, I never gave permission for that." Crawford's face turned into a sad jack-o-lantern. His eyes studied something on the floor until I said, "Well, I guess it will be okay. I'll talk to his mother to see if you can stay until we return."

Crawford gave me a quick hug and ran out the front door to find Davie and tell him the good news. I turned my attention to Charles, "Most of the boarders are gone for the holiday, so maybe my friend, Jane, will be able to handle the boarding house alone while we go to the party, but you have to get me back home as soon as possible. No hangover the next morning, if you get my meaning."

Charles grinned. "Does this mean we can book only one room?" He pulled me into a hug and kissed my neck, moving his lips up to find my mouth. I melted into his embrace. Maybe this get-away was just the thing I needed. Charles and I hadn't had the chance to be intimate since we had returned to the boarding house. If I could get him to reduce his excessive consumption of alcohol, he would be a good candidate for marriage.

The day before New Years Day, the morning began with a cold northwest wind. My mood reflected the dark rolling clouds that moved in from the north, perhaps foretelling the dark events to come. At least the first snow had been slight, so we could use the buckboard rather than the sleigh, which was a slower ride. Oblivious to my mood, Charles sang a merry tune as he made preparations for travel. We dressed in our warmest clothes, and I warmed the soap stones to place under our feet. Charles packed the back of the buckboard with our travel bags, then came back in, stomping his feet by the door.

"Josie, where are the lap blankets you use for traveling in winter? I've got everything else packed, but I don't know where those are. I'll put the soap stones for our feet in right before we leave. I need some rags to wrap them in, too."

That man was clueless, but he did make life interesting. At times, he could make me laugh even when I didn't feel like laughing. However, the drunkenness had to stop. While we were away at Kankakee, I planned to talk to him about going to Dickey Sanitarium in Shelby to get the Dickey Remedy. I had seen a pamphlet promising to cleanse the nerve cells of all sediments and to remove all desire for liquor and to build up the entire system. The twenty-five-dollar sanitarium stay included first-class accommodations, hot-cold baths, and barber service. It sounded wonderful, if only I could get Charles to agree to go.

I could deal with social drinking, in fact, I enjoyed a drink occasionally just as much as the next person, but Charles' drinking was getting out of hand. I couldn't have him spend time with Crawford if he was drunk all the time. I made up my mind that if he didn't change, I would stop seeing him. Thinking of Crawford came first and foremost. I didn't want him to look at Charles as his role model.

The trip to Kankakee chilled us to the bone. We piled on all the blankets we had brought, and the soap stones at our feet began to cool after several miles. Our teeth chattered as we tried to talk, so Charles produced a flask. "Take a swallow of this. It'll warm you up."

Frowning at him, I took a big swallow, then tossed it out the side of the buckboard into the thick wooded area next to the road. Charles grabbed my arm and twisted it hard. "What'd you do that for?" His dark eyes seemed to cut right through my chest. Trying to keep Charles from drinking was not my best choice. I hadn't seen this side of him before. Maybe making a clean break was the answer.

I was too cold to begin a conversation about the loss of the flask, so I said, "I don't want you to drink while we're traveling. You can't control the horses as well."

Quiet settled over the rest of our trip and I brightened when we finally arrived in Kankakee. Charles signed us in, as Mr. and Mrs. Rainey, and I didn't object. After settling into our hotel room, Charles joined his friend, James Rife, to go to the saloon, while promising they would be back in time to take Lizzie Rife and me for dinner downstairs. I crashed on the bed and must have fallen asleep. Hearing a knock at my door, I thought perhaps Charles had forgotten his key, but it was Mrs. Rife. "I think we need to go to the saloon and get our husbands."

I didn't bother to correct her about referring to Charles as my husband. "Come in. What time is it anyway? I must have dozed off."

"I'm so worried. James doesn't drink very often. What if something happened to them?"

After taking a few minutes to freshen up, we walked across the icy street, holding on to one another so we wouldn't slip. When we arrived at the saloon, Charles and James were both quite drunk. It took all we could do to convince them to come back to our rooms. As I helped Charles up the stairs, he repeated several times, "I'm sorry, Josie. I'll make it up to you."

Inside our room, Charles dropped onto the bed, out cold. I went downstairs to get some coffee and a bite to eat, hoping it would sober him up somewhat. Shaking him when I returned, I said, "Charles, drink this. Maybe it will help make you feel better."

Looking down at this man I thought I cared for with his alcoholic breath and loss of any useful muscles, I couldn't wait to go home, but I knew he would still want to attend the New Year's dance the next day when he felt better, and I didn't have any other means of transportation, so I was stuck. Why did I ever agree to this trip?

Because of the drafty cold air coming in through the cracks around the window of the hotel room, I decided to curl up under the covers on the other side of the bed. Charles wouldn't be waking any time soon, anyway. But sleep was as elusive as a woodland rabbit and when I did sleep, I dreamed of Jim's untimely death. Unrested, I woke and moved to the chair so I could look out the window at the soft falling snow in the moonlight.

In the morning, Charles woke up full of apologies. He promised after the party he would quit drinking. "Josie, it will be my New Year's resolution. But tonight, let's just have a good time. That's what we came here for, right?"

His wide smile softened me. Believing in this man was my weakness. I didn't comment but got a kettle of warm water from the atop the wood stove to get cleaned up from our previous day's travel. I started to unbutton my dress and saw Charles approaching out of the corner of my eye. He pulled my hands to my sides and finished unbuttoning my dress bodice and loosening my corset. His touch awoke what I had been missing. My fingers shook as I worked to lift his shirt above his head and pull his trousers loose. He pulled me towards the bed and flopping down together, our bodies joined in with what I hoped would be the promise of a future full of love.

That night after meeting the Rife's for dinner in the hotel dining room, we moved to the dance hall to welcome the new year. A large group had already assembled in the saloon. Most of the tables held several party goers, but Charles managed to spot one that still had four available seats. A small band consisting of a fiddler, an accordion player and another young man who played the harmonica kept the music flowing in between champaign toasts to anything the rowdy bunch thought worth mentioning for the upcoming year.

Attempting to make the dance a formal affair, the men sported dark suits with white shirts and the women wore their finest silk evening gowns. Charles looked so handsome in his attire. Along with his navy suit he added a bright blue tie and a shiny belt buckle. My light blue evening dress complimented his choice of color.

Charles took my hand and led me to the end of the line of couples facing one another to dance the next reel. Many of the women stole glances at my handsome partner, but they'd be surprised to know what was hiding beneath his dark visage. Sometimes I wondered if I was wasting my time with this untamable man.

After each dance, Charles went to the bar for more drinks for the four of us. On a recent trip, I grabbed his arm and insisted, "Don't buy anymore for me. One of us needs to stay sober."

When he came back with another drink for me, I tried giving him a disapproving look, but he smiled, gave me a kiss and dragged me out to dance again. As the evening continued, Charles drank more and danced less. Our last attempt ended with me holding him up and then guiding him to sit down at our table. There he stayed for the rest of the evening after ordering a bottle of whisky. When James refused to drink anymore, I asked the Rife's to help me get Charles back to our room. Between the three of us, we managed to help him cross the street and got him up the stairs to our hotel room. Charles sprawled across the bed, unconscious of his surroundings and how he got there.

Turning from that scene, I stepped close to Charles' friends. "Thank you. I'm sorry Charles spoiled our evening."

Lizzie took my hand. "I'm sorry to leave you like this. We've got quite a drive tomorrow and need to get some sleep."

"We'll be fine. I'm going to get Charles a cup or two of coffee. Maybe that will help to sober him up."

When I returned Charles was sitting on the side of the bed holding his head in his hands. I handed him the coffee. "I feel like hell. Thanks, maybe this will help. As soon as the sun comes up, we're heading for home." He tried to grab my arm, but I moved away. He drank the coffee, and I poured him another cup. His red, blotchy face showed no handsome features now. After relieving himself in the chamber pot, I helped him get his shoes and jacket off and get under the covers. I crawled into the bed on the other side knowing I was safe, considering the shape he was in.

In the morning, I offered to get us some breakfast, but he kept twisting around, rubbing his stomach and proclaiming that he still felt like hell.

"Are you going to throw up that whiskey?" I went to find a slop bucket just in case. Back inside the room his groans had intensified, and he kept writhing and twisting around like he was in misery. Finally, he just straightened up and sat a moment, then fell right back and died. He had thrown up a little bit of foam, so I wiped his mouth and combed his hair. Feeling numb, all I wanted to do was leave for home, but first, I needed to report this to the constable.

Chapter 11: 1885

I have never been one to shed many tears, so I went back down to the dining room and announced in an uncaring voice, "Charles Rainey just died in our room upstairs. Could someone go get the constable?"

Little did I understand that not showing any emotion would add fuel to the rumors that started almost before Charles' dead face was covered with a sheet. People were astonished that such a young man had died so unexpectedly and for no apparent reason except for a ripsnorter of a two-day drunk.

The constable questioned me, and I repeated my story of the odd way Charles had straightened up and fell back dead. Dr. Tinker arrived and examined the body in our upstairs rented room. He marked the death as of natural causes.

After Constable Dunham spent my valuable time questioning me twice more, I began to worry about the trip home. "It's starting to snow, and I'd like to be on my way before the snow gets too deep. Is there any way I can take Charles' body back to Momence soon? I need to get home to my son."

After wrapping poor Charles in several blankets and securing them with rope, I enlisted the help of two strong boys to place him in the back of the buckboard along with our belongings and I made the cold, lonely trip back to Momence. The snowstorm held off and I returned with no problem, but the cold temperatures continued, and the ground remained too frozen for burial. We had to keep his body tied high in the livery stable for several weeks. After several days of thawing in the middle of February, the other boarders and I were able to bury Charles properly.

Without a man who demanded too much of my attention, Crawford and I again relied on one another. I busied myself trying to improve the meals for the boarders who remained, and Crawford helped as much as he could when he wasn't in school. I had almost put the awful experience of Charles' death out of my mind when one afternoon Deputy Stephens showed up at the boarding house after riding all the way to Momence to serve me a warrant demanding my appearance in Kankakee.

"What's this?" I asked, looking at the paper now in my hand.

Stevens explained in a timid voice. "The coroner arrived after you left and found a small brown bottle containing a liquid. It was on the floor in the room you and the deceased had occupied, and chemical tests showed it was strychnine poison." He stopped to clear his throat. "Also, traces of residue in the bottom of the coffee cup proved to contain the same poison."

Clutching the doorframe, I protested, "I don't know anything about any poison. Besides, I don't have to honor this. You're out of your jurisdiction."

"Sorry, Mrs. McKnight, but if you don't appear at court, you're probably going to end up in jail."

After thinking this over for several days, I decided I needed to clear my name for Crawford's sake. Not knowing how long I would need to stay in Momence, I gave notice to the rest of my boarders that I would be selling the house. It had been difficult to remain in that house ever since I returned from Kankakee. Every time I thought of Charles and me spending time there together, my stomach flip-flopped faster than a butter churn. As a result, I'd been having trouble sleeping. I needed to move on. Once I sold the boarding house, my goal became returning to Riley's Grove to develop my inherited property near Willow Lake.

My luck increased when the owner of the saloon decided he would like to expand his holdings in the town and offered me a fair sum for the boarding house. I sent a notice to Isom and asked if he could please load my belongings, all stored now in the bedroom Crawford and I shared and put them in the cabin where Jim and I had lived. That life now seemed like a very long time ago. Dad was excited that we would be back into his fold, but I wondered how long it could last. Life there was drastically different now that mother was gone.

Before returning to Willow Lake, Crawford and I traveled to Kankakee so I could check in with the constable. We booked a room at the hotel across the street from the one where Charles and I stayed. The stares from the guests and manager at the hotel where Charles died would have been too much for me to handle. The next day, I enrolled Crawford in St. Joseph's Seminary for boys to continue his schooling, making sure he was settled before I reported to the constable.

Constable Dunham met me at the door of his office when I arrived bright and early the following morning. "Come in Josie. Have a seat."

"I'll stand if you don't mind. I'm sure this won't take long."

Dunham sat down behind his big desk and began to rub his chin. He leaned back on the rear two legs of his chair and his big belly nearly burst through his waistcoat. "Certain witnesses have testified that you and Charles had been arguing heavily on the night in question. And there's the matter of the brown bottle that was found to hold strychnine. What do you have to say about all that?"

Walking back and forth the length of the office I answered, "I admit we had been arguing. But, as far as the brown bottle is concerned, I never saw it. Maybe Charles got it mixed up with some of the medicine he was taking or maybe he thought it contained whisky. I didn't see him do it, but he must have poured it in his coffee by mistake. Or maybe he was intending to poison me. Did you ever think of that?"

Dunham flopped his chair back down on all fours with a loud bang, frazzling my nerves even more. "So, you're telling me you don't know anything about the poison and how it got in the cup of coffee? Is that correct?"

"Yes. If I was angry enough to get rid of Charles Rainey, I would have lived up to my reputation and grabbed a gun and shot him, like people claim I did to my first husband, which I didn't do, by the way. He died after leaning against the banister and falling to his death, not from my bullet. But people are still claiming I killed him." My voice rose a notch. "Yessir, that's what I should have done. Besides, do you think I would have packed poison along on our trip where Charles could have found it?"

Constable Dunham smiled at my outburst. "I've heard the rumors about you killing your husband. I think if you really wanted Rainey dead, you probably would have found a way that wouldn't point back to you." Dunham steepled his fingers over his chest and cleared his throat, "Besides, the Rife's and a few others spoke in your favor and said there was no way you could have poisoned Charles." He stood then, as if to indicate his questioning had ended. "But just in case, stick around a few days until the judge has a chance to review the testimony and decides if we need to have a trial."

I returned to my room at the hotel. At dinner that night in the hotel dining room, I sat alone near a table of six guests. A loud-speaking young man was talking about an upcoming hanging in the nearby town of Rensselaer. I couldn't help but overhear.

When they got up to leave, I asked him, "Excuse me, I couldn't help but hear. Can you tell me why they are hanging the poor fellow?"

The young man replied as he made his way out of the room, "Killed a man called Dreger in cold blood."

Not that dear young man who had rented a room from me. Going into the lobby of the hotel, I purchased a newspaper, The Kankakee Daily Times. When back in my room, I scanned the paper, but I didn't need to look far. The headlines read, 'Hanging of Weibern Wartena Postponed.' The story went on to describe how "Wartena, age 39, a husband and father of three from Friesland had moved to DeMotte, a few miles south of the Kankakee River. A young German neighbor, John Dreger, a widower for only two years, lived alone, not far from the Wartena's. He took pity on Wartena's poor Dutch family by bringing fresh milk for the children. Both being fishermen, Wartena enticed the young man to go fishing with him at the Kankakee River. After reaching a secluded spot, Wartena bludgeoned Dreger to death with the butt of a rifle." My insides turned into mush. I liked Dreger when he rented the room from me. What a tragedy.

The story went on, "After the murder, Wartena tied two old iron pumps to the corpse and used Dreger's own horses to drag him to the river. The murder would have gone undiscovered if another fisherman, Lorenzo Brainard, hadn't found Dreger's body floating in the river. The iron weights had not been heavy enough to keep the corpse submerged. Jasper County Sheriff, Samuel Yeoman arrested Wartena in November 1884 and took him to the jail in Rensselaer."

When I read that story, I felt compelled to go to witness the hanging. I wanted justice for poor Dreger. And in my mind, except for a few helpful witnesses, this could be me who would be hanged.

After several days, Constable Dunham contacted me to say that I was free to go. There would be no inquest, and no charges would be filed. I breathed a sigh of relief and made my way to St. Joseph's Seminary to explain to Crawford we could now return to Riley's Grove after finalizing business in Momence.

The school's brick dormitory housed all the boys who attended St. Joseph's. But since classes were in session, I instead entered the classroom building. Ivy partially covered the brick, and the white-frame windows gave a cheery look to the large structure. Sister Evangeline emerged from her small office when I entered the foyer. After explaining my reason for visiting, she called for Crawford to come out of class to meet me. His first words were, "Do I have to leave? I like being with all these boys."

Sister Evangeline smiled. "Crawford has adjusted very well here. We'd love to have him stay."

Even though I'd miss him terribly, knowing Crawford liked the school, it cleared my way to go back to Momence to finish the sale of the boarding house and return to Riley's Grove without worrying about the continuation of his schooling.

The sale of the boarding house went well and after signing the paperwork, I rode to Riley's Grove, planning to scope out my property, and maybe do a little digging for the gold again. Dad met my carriage as I drove up to the main house.

"Josie, we're so happy you were able to come back home." My father looked haggard. Lots of gray now interlaced with his dark hair. "Lizzie and I have missed you. Where's Crawford?"

When had she gone from Elizabeth to Lizzie? Dad had given her a more intimate name in my absence. "Crawford is at St. Joseph's. He begged me to stay. Says he loves being with all the boys."

"Going to miss having him around. You're planning to stay though, right? Isom delivered all your things to the cabin like you asked and Lizzie and her helpers have been cleaning and arranging it all for you to move in."

My mouth must have dropped open, and I felt my insides heat. "She went through my things?"

"Now don't go getting all riled up. They just made it so you can get in there. Isom just stacked everything wherever. You wouldn't have been able to move around."

Feeling obstinate, I spent the day rearranging what Lizzie had done. The next morning, I rode out to my Willow Lake property. It was disappointing to see the many sloughs filled with water from the early spring rains. The big ditch had drained most of the lake, but these slight depressions stubbornly kept the area from becoming completely tillable land. Imagining a future for this property had to include a way to dry it out. For the moment, I set those thoughts aside and proceeded to dig in a few more spots for Shatner's gold. No luck again.

Chapter 12

Bailey looked up from her notes. "That was quite a story. I can't believe they thought you might have poisoned Charles."

"I did get out of that by the skin of my teeth. It was good riddance to Charles, though. I don't think he was ever going to give up drinking for me."

"Aunt Josie, did you ever find that gold?"

"Oh, I'll never tell that part of my story." Aunt Josie slapped her knees and laughed. "Maybe I did and maybe I didn't. The big story you should write about in your next article is the hanging. That was quite something for these parts. I never saw so many people all in one spot in my entire life. Maybe they have some old newspapers at the library so you can do some research and get all the facts straight. My mind is not as clear as it used to be."

"I will do that, but right now can you tell me what you remember about it?"

1886

Staying at Riley's Grove and seeing my father dote on Lizzie, fostered a restlessness in my soul I couldn't explain. I had thought this was the answer to my anxiety, being where my dear mother had lived, but those memories were now stained with Lizzie's presence. At least I had the cabin to myself, but being there turned my thoughts to my marriage to Jim and its terrible end. I began spending days out at the Willow Lake property, where I spent the time focusing on my plans for the area. I even staked out some plots, dividing the property into smaller units, one hundred sixty and three hundred twenty acres each. However, I found it difficult to ride in a straight line to place the flags on the corners of the plots. I'd have to hire professional surveyors to complete the partitioning. My vision was for each farm to have its own equipment, horses, implements and livestock and with luck, I'd be able to find individuals who would be willing to work the land and share the profits with me. A community of like-minded workers would be the result. Unfortunately, all my plans would have to wait for now since the land still was too wet to farm.

In October, Dad decided to host a party for his sixty-fourth birthday. It seemed to give him a renewed look on life, so I supported his decision. Gen. Logan, a candidate for U.S. Senator, greeted over one thousand people at the barbeque, held at Riley's Grove. The fine weather made the day a treat, but the roads were bad, and parties had to travel seven miles from the railroad station in the muddy mess.

Even the Chicago Tribune reported on the party. Dad was at the height of his glory. I hadn't seen him so happy in several years. Our relationship improved again after the party, and I tried to get along better with Lizzie, also.

Helping my father as much as possible with the running of the homestead, the next couple months flew by while at Riley's Grove. In the evening, I would eat dinner with my father and Elizabeth. At one of these meals, we discussed the upcoming hanging.

"Dad, have you heard any more about when the hanging will take place?"

"No. Why are you so interested? You don't need to go running off to see that hanging."

Shoveling another bite into my mouth, I didn't respond to Dad's directive. My mind turned again to the death of poor Dreger. He had been such a good person to deal with at the boarding house, always willing to help out with any chores. How awful to be the victim of murder when only trying to do what was right.

Becoming bored with my life at Riley's Grove, I decided I couldn't continue to live there. It just wasn't home anymore, and I didn't want to miss the excitement of the hanging. I needed to find more news about it, so I could be there when the hanging took place. Just to be safe, I planned to move after the upcoming Christmas holidays when Crawford would move back to school.

Several years ago, when Mother's illness kept Dad close, he had arranged with the Star Route mail carrier to make a special stop at Riley's Grove. Even after mother died, my father made it worthwhile for the carrier to continue delivering the mail, so we didn't have to pick it up in town. There was much excitement whenever he rode up.

Just after the new year, while I helped with the laundry, I heard dad's call, "Mail's here."

Receiving mail prompted everyone to step outside briefly. The mail carrier handed me a letter from Crawford and gave Dad the newspaper from Kankakee. "Got time for a cup of coffee, Hank?" Dad asked while running his hand down the horse's flank, trying to release the tension it displayed after running for such a long distance.

"No sir, got to make it to Rensselaer by afternoon. The judge there is waiting for some letter from the lawyer for that fellow, Wartena."

Perking up my ears, I snatched the newspaper from Dad's hand and ran inside to sit at the table to read. According to the recent newspaper story, the judge had rescheduled the hanging after Wartena's second trial conviction. The date was now set for Friday, February 26th. The article went on to state that "on the day of the execution, the lucky parties possessing tickets will be admitted in to see Wartena while he lays on his bunk previous to the fixed hour and be allowed in the hanging enclosure to view the execution." Being that close did not interest me, but going to the hanging was something I couldn't pass up.

Also, after thinking about it for weeks, I had decided staying in Rensselaer after witnessing the hanging might be the best solution to my dilemma of where I could next fit in.

When I made Dad aware of my plans, he shook his head. "Do what you have to do, girl. Just don't forget, this is your real home."

Waiting until the weather improved somewhat, I again enlisted Isom's help to load my carriage with a few items of furniture along with several trunks of clothing and household items just in case I would be able to find a suitable property to buy in Rensselaer.

On the day I left the farm, the melting snow and bright sunshine made me excited to be on the move. Dad held me close and whispered, "Josie, I'm going to miss you. It's never the same when you and Crawford aren't here." He held me at arm's length so I could see his face, and I'll never forget how much older he seemed at that moment. He added, "And I promise I'll find a way to make your land usable. Then you'll have to come back."

The unusually busy roadway made for a slow trip from Riley's Grove to Rensselaer, especially with the muddy conditions from the melting snow. I had estimated the drive to take about four hours, but having to stop several times to let horse riders and smaller buggies pass extended the time quite substantially. It seemed all of the northern Indiana settlers had the same idea as I did.

Arriving in the town, the amount of activity alarmed me. How would I ever find a room for the night? I pulled up under a large sign advertising the law office of Morris and Lumas. The tinkling sound of a bell above the door when I opened it made the lone occupant look up from his desk and stare my way. "Can I help you?"

"I need legal advice. My name is Josie McKnight. I'm from Riley's Grove."

The man's broad smile and welcoming brown eyes made me feel at home at once. He was several years my senior but had kept his youthful looks by remaining trim and dressing in a fashionable vest and jacket. His well-kept mustache curved up toward both cheeks even more when he smiled. I extended my hand, and it surprised me how firm his handshake felt. He held my hand in his several more moments, then said, "What sort of legal advice does a beautiful young lady like you need?"

Turning my head so Mr. Morris wouldn't see my heated cheeks, the clamor outside held my attention for a moment before I answered. "My, this is a big event, isn't it?" I walked to the window of his office to watch as more buggies, people on horses and foot traffic filled the street. "I don't suppose you know of any house I could purchase so I could open a boarding house here?" Turning to see his reaction, he smiled at me again.

"Yes, we don't often have a hanging in our town." He joined me at the window and spoke looking out. "I have just the house. Actually, it's my house, but it's way too large for one person. I've been meaning to open it up for renters but just haven't made work of it. I hope you don't judge me as being too forward, but an idea popped into my head that will benefit us both. I don't want to sell the house, but you could manage the renting of rooms for me and make the meals for my boarders. With all the people in town for the hanging on Friday, we could do a great business."

"Show me this grand house. You might have just gotten yourself a business partner, Mr. Morris."

"It's George, if you feel so inclined."

George joined me in my carriage and grabbed the reins, but I wasn't sure I liked how he took over. After all, I was used to taking care of myself. Then realizing how difficult it was to maneuver the busy streets; I appreciated sitting back and watching the crowds. We drove up to a large, beautifully painted house with decorative brackets, lace-like detailing, and intricate trim work. The ornate construction details extended onto the porch railings and columns, extending the width of the house. I fell in love with it. Stealing a glance at George, I decided, perhaps its owner wasn't too bad either.

"This is perfect. I'd like to get started right away."

Laughing, George said, "You and I don't waste any time, do we? Looks like we have a deal." He shook my hand and again he held it a few seconds longer than necessary.

George approached some young teens who had congregated on the corner near the house and paid them to carry my belongings into the small room in the back near the kitchen where I would lodge. Then he went somewhere else into the house and came out with a painted sign stating, 'Rooms for Rent.' He attached it to a post near the road and went to stable my horse. By eight that evening every room in the large upstairs had been taken. Exhausted, I turned in early, so George and I didn't have more chance to talk.

After preparing a hearty breakfast for our new boarders the next morning, I took a stroll to see the rest of the town and perhaps find more provisions. On foot I could witness the assemblage firsthand. The would-be spectators who couldn't find a room had camped in their buggies or slept on blankets on the ground even though the temperature had dropped to the low forties. At the hotel, a line of those waiting to purchase some breakfast and warm up, broke out from the door and descended onto the steps. The whole town was bursting with activity like a sudden Midwest rainstorm. Turning my attention to the distant sound of the Chicago and Indianapolis Railway engine heading toward the Rensselaer station, I followed the noise toward the depot. The steam engine pulled in with loud hissing and squeaking brakes. Before long the conductor called for the doors to open and visitors crowded out onto the platform, seeming bewildered at the sea of humanity.

At the end of the platform, a man standing up in his buckboard, waved his arms wanting attention. When I realized it was George, I hurried to leave the crowded train station and climbed up to sit next to him. "This town has gone crazy, and the hanging isn't until Friday."

George clicked to the horses and we moved away from all the hubbub. "I made sure to get plenty of supplies. I was afraid they'd sell out. Let's get them and you back to safety."

George kept busy at his office on Thursday, and I only saw him for dinner that night. On Friday everyone woke early wanting to get a good view of the proceedings, so the house cleared out as soon as we finished breakfast. George and I went to his office where we would have a great view of the show and sat together on a bench in front of the building. At eleven thirty Sheriff Yeoman let those with tickets into the inner area close to the gallows. The procession made its way from Wartena's cell to the gallows near the courthouse with two clergy leading the way, and Wartena and the sheriff following behind. After walking up the steps of the gallows, Wartena stood with the noose already around his neck. The sheriff boomed, "Got any last words to say?"

Wartena yelled out in broken English, "I'm innocent. May God have mercy on my accusers."

George grasped my hand as if this was our usual custom and I was happy to accommodate. The sheriff then adjusted the rope and black cap, the trap sprung, and the crowd gasped in unison. Everything worked with precision. The spectacle had become one for the history books. In stunned silence, George and I sat watching the many curiosity seekers who passed by the swinging corpse. After thirty minutes, the sheriff and his men took the body down.

By Saturday morning some of our boarders and most of the visitors who had come to Rensselaer just to view the hanging had headed home. The streets returned to the quiet of a small midwestern town.

Chapter 13

After leaving the library, Bailey hurried back to her house. She wanted to share her findings with her aunt. Out of breath, she rushed into the front parlor. "I found some more information about that Wartena case, Aunt Josie."

Josie laid her knitting down and leaned her head back against the chair. "Let's hear it. I want to see if I remembered everything correctly."

Bailey took a couple deep breaths and began to read from her notes. "In the spring of 1884, the Wartenas, a Dutch family, 'in deep poverty' moved to Keener Township near DeMotte, Indiana, a few miles north of the Kankakee River. Here within six months Wartena murdered their German neighbor, John Dreger. He lived alone, took pity on the indigent Dutch family and befriended them, even bringing fresh milk for the children. The Dutchman enticed Dreger to go fishing in the Kankakee River, and Dreger drove the two to the river with his own team and a borrowed wagon. After reaching a secluded spot on the bank, Wartena bludgeoned Dreger to death with the butt of a pistol. Wartena tied two old iron pumps to the corpse and used the horses to drag it into the river. The murderer then went to Dreger's farm and took everything—horses, cows, and other animals, household goods, and clothing, even his best suit. The schemer tried to cover his tracks by concocting an elaborate tale. He stated that he had purchased Dreger's property for three hundred seventy-five dollars and given him a bank note for four hundred dollars. He said Dreger had gone to Chicago to exchange it to get twenty-five dollars in cash for Wartena. The story sold well for several weeks, until another fisherman found Dreger's body floating in the river. The iron weights had not been enough to keep the bloated corpse submerged."

Josie looked out the near window. "Oh yes, I remember all of that now. It was so sad to see that poor widow at the hanging. She had no way to support herself and her children after his death. I think the Dutch community did help her out, though." Josie sighed, then continued, "That whole incident changed my life forever. I became determined to be self-sufficient and after George died, I might have gone a little overboard."

"Wait a minute. We need to back up. You and George got together? And then he died?

1886-1887

After the hanging, I wrote to both my father and Crawford to let them know I would be staying on in Rensselaer for a while. George kept busy with his law practice, and I continued to manage his boarding house. Each evening after his long hours at the law office, George and I would have a late dinner together. I never ate with the boarders anymore. I made that mistake once before, and it got me into plenty of trouble.

After keeping two plates warm in the oven George and I would sit together in the cozy kitchen at a small table, eating and talking about the day's events. George was always a perfect gentleman. His quiet ways soothed my turbulent soul, and I found myself growing fonder of him each day. In the course of our long talks, I admitted that I had had a rather turbulent love life so far. He didn't seem to mind, in fact George hung on every word as I told him what had happened to both Jim and Charles.

"I was too young when I married Jim and found out later, we were not suited to one another. If he had not died so tragically, I had made up my mind to try to divorce him. With Charles, I suppose I was taken in by his dashing appearance and his eloquent, persuasive manner. I'm sure I would have come to my senses soon after the trip to Kankakee. At least, I like to think that I would have."

Sometimes on the weekend George and I would take long rides ending in a picnic lunch if the spring weather cooperated or we'd attend one of the many traveling theater company's shows presented at the local playhouse, and of course we attended church together on Sunday.

On one of our outings in mid-April 1887, George remained so quiet, I worried he was ill. When we stopped and he helped me down from the carriage, I couldn't contain myself any longer. "Are you sick, George? If so, we can return to town right away."

Before I knew it, George was down on one knee, worrying me even more. I grabbed at his underarm meaning to help him up, but he jerked his arm away. "Josie, can't you see I'm proposing?" My shocked face must have alarmed him enough to stand and brush off his dusty knee. "Oh, forget it. I should have known you wouldn't want to marry such an old fool."

With those words, he climbed back into the carriage and clicked at the horses to turn back for town. I found myself standing there wondering what had just happened. Watching as the carriage disappeared behind a grove of trees, I then started to walk back toward town. But before long, in a cloud of dust, the carriage reappeared, coming toward me with George yelling to the horses to 'giddyap.'

Hurrying towards him, I ran to embrace the man I loved, when he jumped down. "You didn't wait for me to answer. Of course I'll marry you. I've been waiting for you to ask."

George insisted that at his age he didn't want to wait for us to get married. I had no doubts about this marriage being the best thing that had happened to me. So, only two days later, George and I were joined in matrimony in front of a judge at the courthouse in Rensselaer with a couple of George's friends in attendance. I hadn't even had time to send an invitation to my father or get Crawford from his school, so we made plans to drive to both Kankakee and Riley's Grove for our honeymoon so my family could meet George.

~

Crawford was not as overjoyed as I had hoped when we met him in the school's drawing room, and I introduced him to George. I was so disappointed when he asked me if he could spend the evening with his friends instead of joining us for dinner. George had helped me move forward and I wanted to share him with my son.

Later that evening in our hotel room, George took me in his strong arms. "He's only thirteen, Josie. He'll come around when he matures somewhat."

Pulling the horses to a stop in front of the big house at Riley's Grove, my heart continued the thumping sound of the carriage wheels. Taking huge breaths to try to calm down, I took a good look at my new husband. What would my father say about me getting married to this man who was quite a bit older than me? Dad only wanted the best for me, I reminded myself, and George was the best person I knew. Besides, age had not mattered to him, when he went wife hunting.

"What's going on out there?" A voice boomed from behind the carved wooden door when Elizabeth opened it to greet us. To my surprise, Dad was standing in the hall leaning on a cane. Had he aged that much since I had seen him last? I ran to his side for a hug, but he held out his arm. "You'll knock me over, girl. I don't have much balance right now."

I looked to Elizabeth for an explanation, but she was staring at George, evidently at a loss for words again.

"It's just a little sprained ankle. It'll be better in no time." Turning to look at George, Dad continued, "Who have we here, Josie? Another high roller?" Letting out a belly laugh, he leaned on his cane with one hand and held out his other to shake hands with George.

"No sir, I'm Josie's husband." George grabbed Henry's hand, with a hearty shake, nearly pulling him over.

"Well, thank goodness. Looks like she made the right choice this time. You've got a great handshake. Come on into the parlor and have a brandy. Lizzie, please have Lottie make a room ready for our guests."

"Oh Dad, we can stay in the cabin. We don't want to make any fuss."

"How am I supposed to get to know my son-in-law if you're way out there in the cabin?"

George followed my father into the parlor and the two men connected while Elizabeth and I made sure our trunk was carried upstairs to the guest room. I tried to begin a conversation with my father's wife, but I found her to be quite mute again. Taking off my outer cloak and discarding my shoes, I flopped down on the bed, exhausted. The next thing I knew George woke me with the sweetest kisses, his breath smelling like my father's brandy.

Into my neck, he mumbled, "I love it here. Let's move to Riley's Grove."

"My father got to you. You haven't even seen my property. And you've been drinking."

George raised up on his elbow, slurring his words, "Wait, you have property? You never told me that." His usual carefully combed hair fell over his forehead and the knot in his tie had loosened. He pulled it free and began to unbutton his shirt. I didn't answer his question. I just pulled him under the bedcovers to christen the guest bed with our love.

The next morning, I met Dad for coffee before the others came down for breakfast. "You were out of line last night, telling George we could move back to Riley's Grove on my property. Even if I wanted to, George has his practice in Rensselaer. He can't just up and move."

"We've got plenty of legal work for him right around here. Come on, Josie. We need to be a family again."

"I'll think about it, but George will have to decide. Last night he was convinced to move, but it might have been the alcohol talking."

Sitting around the table after lunch, Henry again brought up his wish for them to move to Riley's Grove. "You know, Josie, I'm working on some way to get that limestone shelf cut down so we can get your property drained better. We're going to hire some workers to dig that out so the river can flow freely to the west."

"You're dreaming, Dad. That's going to be impossible."

"Nothing is impossible, right George?"

"Right, Henry."

Josie looked from her husband to her father. Had this coalition been forged in one evening of drinking together? She had to admit, it felt good to have both her men getting along so well. She may as well enjoy this new phase of her life. "George, since you're convinced, we should move, let's take a ride out to my property. You'll see, it's not good for much right now."

Dad laughed and said, "Except a treasure hunt for gold."

George's eyes widened, "Gold?"

"I'll explain on our way there."

Chapter 14: 1888-1893

George and I moved to Riley's Grove in 1888. It had taken nearly a year for George to finish up his cases in Rensselaer, sell his half of the law practice to his partner and find a buyer for the boarding house. In the meantime, we broke ground for a house to be built on Refuge Island in the middle of what had been Willow Lake. Traveling from Rensselaer to Riley's Grove became common for me during that year, with me doing most of the overseeing of the builders' work. I soon earned the reputation of being a stickler for perfection.

The day the workers dug down to place the rock for the foundation, I made sure I was at the site to oversee the work. I wasn't going to have them abscond with my gold if they happened to dig it up during the excavation. Again, I was disappointed. Had old Shatner really buried any gold? At this point it seemed doubtful.

While George and I busied ourselves with building our home, settling in on Refuge Island, and George opening his law office in Laketown, my father was becoming more influential in the fight to drain the rest of the Kankakee River area. He worked tirelessly along with other landowners to convince the state of Indiana to become involved. In May of 1893 the state lawmakers appropriated $65,000 to widen and deepen the main channel near Momence.

Elizabeth invited us to Riley's Grove for dinner saying Henry had big news. Dad was ecstatic at dinner when he relayed the information "The state came through with the money needed for the work in Momence. Now, we'll be able to hire the workers we need to dig out that limestone. The river is low, so it's a perfect time to get this done. I've got fifty workers lined up to start working immediately. All we needed was the state's backing."

In July of 1893, a crew cut a shallow channel not quite a meter deep through the limestone ledge running just east of Momence, which had for millennia partially blocked and restricted the flow of the Kankakee River. But this was only the beginning. A company from St. Paul had been contracted to finish the work and they employed all the help they could get. Boarding places for all the workers added revenue to the businesses in Momence. The town expanded into a small, crowded metropolis for a short time.

Dad fumed when he heard the next bit of news. "Now work has been delayed because a carload of tools from St. Paul got lost in transit. They spent two days trying to trace where the machinery ended up. I don't know if I'll ever see this project completed."

I worried about him. He had little energy for anything except seeing this project through. His other holdings were in good hands, but Dad had always had a finger in everything he started. Now, he spent every day that he could at Momence watching and overseeing the excavation.

It certainly was a sight to watch. Daily blasting required the removal of a huge amount of rock. The rock was piled along the 3I Railroad for later removal. In November the work was completed, and we all made the trip to Momence to watch as the upper dam was opened to allow the river to flow naturally west over what had been the limestone shelf.

Delighted shouts roared out when the river's depth fell dramatically. I turned to look at my father who had tears running down his face. "Josie, this will work wonders for the Kankakee Valley and your property will be usable now. That's what I wanted for you. It's why I worked so hard to get this accomplished."

I hugged him long and hard, but as I did, I felt the thin frame below his clothing. He hadn't been eating enough and the constant traveling to Momence had taken its toll.

"You need to slow down now, Dad, and take a well-deserved rest."

The increased river flow, while doing little for the citizens of Illinois, drained thousands of acres of Indiana wetlands, including more of Dad's twelve thousand acres and my property, permitting more profitable farming. In May of 1894 about seventy-five landowners in the Kankakee Valley met in Chicago to talk over plans for straightening the channel of the Kankakee River in order to secure better drainage for six hundred thousand acres of marsh land.

Unfortunately, Dad was not able to join in this endeavor. After seeing the completion of the project in Momence, Dad didn't have the same energy he had when he was younger. In the fall of 1895, he fell sick with a terrible cold and cough. Most days he stayed in bed, too weak to even come down to the dining room to eat.

From my standpoint, Elizabeth didn't deal well with his illness. She seemed more interested in her preparations for their upcoming Christmas celebration. When Dad called to her from their bed, "Lizzie, I need the bedpan," she would send Janet, the woman she had hired, to deal with the unpleasant situation. Elizabeth had grown so used to being on her own during the days my father had been working on the Momence project that it seemed to me there was now very little love or connection between the two, if there ever had been.

Because of her callousness, my attitude toward Elizabeth became outwardly tolerant for the sake of my father, but inside I hated the woman for the way she was treating him. After spending several days in Kankakee, visiting Crawford and purchasing more décor for our home, I went directly to Dad's room on my return to Riley's Grove. His coughing had gotten worse and after each hacking fit the cloth contained spots of blood. His body shook from a chill, but his forehead indicated an intense fever.

Entering the parlor where Elizabeth sat working on her embroidery, I nearly yelled, "Why haven't you sent for the doctor, Lizzie? You should have had him here days ago."

She looked up, her mouth wide. "Henry insisted we didn't need to bother the doctor. I was afraid he'd be upset with me if I went against his wishes."

"So, you'd prefer to just let him die?" I wanted to slap her indifferent face and make her realize the seriousness of the occasion. Instead, I balled my fists and went to find Isom to send for the doctor.

By the time Dr. Eggert arrived, Dad's breathing had become hurried and with each breath his face contorted in pain. The doctor turned to me after examining him. "Josie, go ask their servant to prepare a poultice with linseed oil."

When I returned to the sick room, Dr. Eggert had administered a dose of Dover's powder and Dad's cough had subsided for a bit.

We wrapped Dad's chest with oiled silk to keep the poultice bound tight and he was finally able to drift off to sleep.

"He needs to drink plenty of milk and broth. Boiled ggs would be great, too. I'll leave some Dover's powder, but don't give it to him unless he's coughing bad again. I'll stop by on my way back from Kankakee in a couple days."

But the next day when I again stopped in to check on Dad, his skin was slightly blue, and his fever had spiked even more. Janet and I sponged his skin with cold water while Elizabeth stood by sniffling. I barked orders. "Make yourself useful and fetch some more cold water."

Elizabeth turned and ran from the room; probably glad she could get away from the scene. What had Dad been thinking when he married such an ineffectual young woman?

By the time Elizbeth returned, Dad's labored breathing filled the room with noisy sucking and wheezing in rapid succession. I continued mopping his brow with the cool water, but again Elizabeth stood back, her face, a mask of horror. Suddenly Dad sat up and pounded his chest as if trying to force the air into himself. Then reaching both arms up for something or someone for a brief moment, he flopped back onto the pillow, and silence filled the room. His labored breathing had stopped, and I knew he was gone from this life. To her credit, Elizabeth flew to the bed, hugged the man who had been her husband these last few years and sobbed into his neck.

Once she cried herself out, she left the room and Janet and I were left to strip the bed and prepare Dad's body for burial. Thankfully the mild December weather made it possible for the men to dig his grave next to mother's in the family plot. George volunteered to get Crawford from school and by the time they pulled into Riley's Grove they had become fast friends. Because Crawford had decided he wanted to become a lawyer, he had peppered George with questions about cases he had tried, and a connection was finally formed.

We received guests for two days with Dad laid out in the parlor, then on Friday we formed a procession following the pallbearers who carried the wooden casket out to the gravesite. The crisp December wind pulled at our outer frocks as we walked, and I hoped the preacher would make quick work of the burial service.

Elizabeth seemed appropriately mournful, her red eyes showing she had shed many tears before the walk to the grave. But as soon as we were heading back, she grabbed my arm and said, "Where am I supposed to be buried? With the grave of the baby between Henry and Margaret, there's no room for me next to Henry. You should have had Henry's grave dug on the other side of Margaret."

I didn't care where Elizabeth would be buried. Actually, I hoped she would move on, now that my dad was gone. I answered with coldness, "Maybe you'll be able to marry again. You're young and then you can be buried with that husband."

Evidently this was something Elizabeth didn't want to hear yet. She started wailing again. "You are an awful person, Josie. I loved your father."

Once the burial was over, my grieving began. Often my thoughts turned to the happy childhood I experienced when my parents were young and so full of life. I tried to concentrate on George and Crawford, but at times my body ached for my mother's touch or conversations I had with my father.

We did not celebrate Christmas with Elizabeth and for the months following Dad's passing, George and I had very little to do with Elizabeth. She continued to knock around in that huge house with only the servants to keep her company.

Chapter 15: 1894

After Christmas, George and I drove Crawford back to Kankakee to finish his studies. He planned to stay at school through the summer to begin studying for his law degree. Although I would miss him, I refrained from expressing anything that could be perceived as sadness about his decision to stay to pursue a legal career.

Again, we bundled up for the cold trip, but this time instead of an open buckboard, we rode in style in a closed carriage. I snuggled into the back seat while George and Crawford claimed the front, taking turns keeping me company in the back and alternating taking turns driving the horses.

As we traveled, I looked out at the large trees along the Kankakee River. Their long black branches exhibited blankets of snow, then joining with the snowy north face of their trunks, making them look like giant skeletons. Some leaf-clad trees wilted with the covering of fluffy clouds of snow and looked like huge snow people. Snowy individuals filled this winter wonderland.

The horses' snorts sounded louder because of the cold weather as they tried to keep an easy pace, and the slight swaying of the carriage calmed my inner being. Sitting comfortably, wrapped in my blanket, I let my thoughts flow back over the last few months, trying to remember all the conversations I had had with my dad. I wanted to follow the same practical methods my father had used on his farm. George and I had decided we would divide our acreage into smaller units just like my father had done. This seemed like the best practice to manage a large tract of farmland like ours. I couldn't wait to take over my father's many investments and expand his methods into our Willow Lake property.

After a while the gentle movement of the carriage and the steady footsteps of the horses nearly lulled me to sleep. I vaguely heard George and Crawford, on the front seat, bantering about their similar career choices. Crawford's excitement bubbled over when discussing his future. "Do you think I could get into one of the law firms in Chicago as an intern next summer? Do you know anyone there who could put in a word for me?"

"Slow down, now. First, you have to get your law degree under your belt, but I'll start sending out some feelers to some of the attorneys I went to school with who ended up in Chicago."

"Mom, did you hear that? George might help me get into a law firm in Chicago."

George's laugh rang out into the cold air. That ended my chance of taking a much-needed nap. "Yes, that's wonderful, Crawford."

My mind started working on possibilities again. Once we dropped Crawford off at his school, we intended to meet with my father's attorney and after that, we were invited to my boarding school friend, Patsy's home for dinner. The excitement of the upcoming events whirred through my mind, and I gave up trying to sleep. Listening to my guys up front again made me grateful I had found a man like George and married him, considering my other two failed relationships. George had become the father-figure Crawford needed, especially now that his grandfather would no longer be around to guide him.

After stopping occasionally to dig the carriage out of a snowbank, we arrived in Kankakee around noon. Crawford's friends met us outside his dorm and grabbed his trunks and valises so quickly it seemed like a whirlwind had just passed. The knowledge that he wouldn't be returning home for an extended period, due to his subsequent plans to pursue a legal career in Chicago after obtaining his law degree, rendered this farewell particularly difficult. I tried not to show how upset I was to leave him, especially in front of his friends, but inside, my heart felt as if it might split in two.

From that bittersweet good-bye, we turned back toward the main street of Kankakee to our appointment with Dad's attorney, William Bastian. Mr. Bastian's office was built to impress. He greeted us from behind his large oak desk. Some sort of typing machine sat on the corner with stacks of law books and papers spread on the rest of the desk top. The wall behind it held a large, oak letter file and shelves of more law books filled the side wall. An iron safe stood in one corner and in the opposite corner stood a pot-bellied stove with a roaring fire burning inside. Three electric lamps hung from the ceiling, lighting the space.

Mr. Bastian motioned for us to sit across from him in the two chairs positioned facing him. He started business immediately. "This is not an official meeting for the distribution of property because Henry's widow, Elizabeth, is not here…"

I interrupted, "Why would she need to be here?"

Mr. Bastian wiped his brow with a hanky. "Well, Mrs. Morris, I'm afraid, since she was Henry's wife, she will inherit all of his holdings unless you can produce a will stating otherwise. Henry did not follow my advice and prepare a legal will. He kept putting it off. Guess he thought he was going to live longer than he did."

My stomach clenched into a knot. What had my father done? To calm my nerves, I rose from my chair to pace and ended up in front of the stove. I stared at the flames in a daze. George asked a few more questions, but I was too upset to zero in on what the two men were saying. The next thing I knew, George took my arm. "Let's go, Josie. There's nothing more we can do here today."

We thanked Mr. Bastian for his time and as we walked out the door, George said loud enough for Bastian to hear, "Don't worry, Josie, I think we can stop this from happening."

I trusted George, but I wondered what he'd have to do to get it done. He wouldn't do anything illegal, but twisting an arm wasn't beyond his scope of activities. Once back in the carriage my anger bubbled up like a volcano ready to erupt. "This can't be happening. My mother and father worked their whole lives to build their businesses. And now Lizzie will end up with it? It's just not right."

George took my hand, "The first thing we'll do is talk to Elizabeth. Maybe she'll be decent about this. I know for a fact; she doesn't need the money. Her family is well supplied."

~

Patsy's large home reminded me of the house we had left in Rensselaer. The beautiful grillwork and lovely colors made it a welcome sight after the disappointment of the afternoon. She had married her childhood sweetheart whose family ran the main bank in the city. Steven and Patsy had four children, all teenagers now. After eating together in their spacious dining room, the boys asked to be excused for a game of football in the snow with the other neighborhood boys and the two girls asked if they could go to their rooms to read. Grabbing dessert from the large, ornate serving buffet, they left, making a quiet void in the large room.

Once the children were gone, we began to tell our dear friends about the predicament that had developed concerning my inheritance. I could barely keep my tears back as I described the turn of events. Ending my story, I said, "I know my father intended for me to inherit his businesses. He often talked to me about his decisions in the last couple years so I would know how to take over."

Tears trickled down my cheeks, and I felt George's arm encircle my shoulders. "If for some reason Elizabeth wants compensation for the return of the property to Josie, we'll need funding. Hopefully, you'll be able to help us with that, Steven."

Silence again enveloped the dining table. I wiped my eyes to see both Patsy and Steven with downcast eyes. Had we overstepped the boundaries with our friends? Maybe their business wasn't as secure as we had hoped.

Steven cleared his throat. "It's not that we don't want to help, but I'm not in charge of the bank yet. My father still holds the reins. He will require collateral if you want to borrow that much money."

No one stirred until Patsy clapped her hands in excitement. Sitting up tall, she said, "I have an idea. Josie, remember how many of our friends who live in Chicago still wanted to own horses. They were always looking for a place to board their animals for a time. Did you ever think about starting that business? It would bring in some short-term capital."

I shoved my chair back, stood and went around the table to give Patsy a hug. She also stood and we rocked back and forth in each other's arms, laughing. I looked at George for his approval. His furrowed brow didn't make me feel very confident. A horse boarding business would never make the funds needed to buy out Elizabeth, but wanting to appreciate Patsy's attempt to help, I would try her idea.

"Patsy, I can always count on you to come up with a solution. Will you help me write letters to all our classmates?"

The next morning, letters in hand, I boarded the train to Chicago to drum up business for our new venture. George planned to talk to Elizabeth on his way home and begin working on the legal angles if she would not cooperate. The future looked a little brighter as I watched the Illinois countryside pass by as I traveled north to Chicago. The white carpet covered every aspect of the view as persistent snowflakes swirled past my window, looking like sparkling pearls.

While in Chicago, I would also attend the International Livestock Show. George insisted I meet with one of his colleagues there who raised old-fashioned Spotted Poland-China pigs. He brought them from his home in Miami County, Ohio, where they originated and was making a great living from the breeding and raising of these animals. George had the hair-brained idea the pigs could be what we needed to make our farm pay and fulfill our dream of making the land become the means to our future wealth. I was not so sure I could handle the sullied aspects of raising hogs, but at this point I would try anything to make Willow Lake productive.

Chapter 16: 1895-1897

When I returned to Riley's Grove, George met my carriage, looking somewhat distressed. Before I could even say hello, he took me in his arms and said, "I'm so sorry, Josie. Elizabeth won't budge about the inheritance and has refused our payment offer. But I don't want you to worry. I've already filed a lawsuit to regain what's rightfully yours."

We walked to our home arm in arm, and I felt a calm return to my spirit, just being close to George and absorbing the lovely fresh air at Willow Lake. Our new hired hand followed behind, carrying my valises. "Just set them here in the foyer, Josiah, we can carry them upstairs later."

Anxious to keep the discussion going with George, I hung up my outer wrap and ushered him into the parlor. The fire roared in the hearth, making flickering shadows on the flowered wall covering and on the red velvet cushions on the chairs and settees. Putting my arms around George's neck, I cooed, "I missed you. Next time I go to Chicago, I want you to come, too."

George pulled at his mustache. "Next time? What went on there that you'll need to return?"

Grabbing George by the hand, I pulled him with me near the settee in front of the fire. "It's the most exciting place. There's activity everywhere. I made many contacts that will help with our livestock business, and we'll need to speak to them again in the future face to face."

We sat down in front of the fire facing the ornately carved walnut mantel. Oval portraits of mother and father hung on either side of the pastoral scene above the fireplace. This room was my favorite in our home. I snuggled against George.

"Now, I want you to bring me up to speed on your visit with

Elizabeth."

"Well, like I said, Elizabeth thinks she will be fine with running the farm. I stressed to her how difficult it would be to do it on her own, but she's naïve and immature. She won't want the responsibility of running that place once she realizes the work that's involved. But, just in case, I went ahead and filed a lawsuit, claiming you are the one entitled to the property near to Willow Lake. It will square off our parcel, increasing our property to seven thousand acres. We'll have to accept that, I'm afraid. Requesting all the property would probably keep us from getting any. The judge will rule on our motion next month."

"Whatever you think will convince the judge. I trust your judgement, George. Regardless." I reached for his hand. "It won't matter in the long run. I had lots of time to think on the train. I've got big plans for Willow Lake. You were so right about raising pigs. With them, there's a much shorter return on our investment than with cattle. Mr. Janes is going to sell us two bred sows to start our herd. He predicts they should each have fourteen to sixteen piglets. Those births will start our new hog business. With this new venture, we'll be able to make our own way without Elizabeth. Also, I have several people that want to board their horses here. They're bringing them next weekend."

"Josie, we don't have any place to keep them." George got up and paced.

"Don't worry. I'll take care of everything. You just keep working on the legal side."

The next day, after a lifetime of dressing in skirts, I switched to wearing pants. Enlisting the help of Josiah, we rode to Riley's Grove to try to hire my father's men to build a corral. The January thaw would make it possible to wedge the posts far enough into the ground to hold the cross beams. They could be dug further into the ground in the spring. This would make the corral would be secure enough to contain the horses I would be boarding. When we arrived at the homestead, I told the men I would pay them half-again as much as they were making. The exodus from the bunkhouse was immediate.

Just as we were ready to ride, Elizbeth drove up in my father's carriage and stopped, wet snow and mud spinning from the wheels. "What do you think you're doing, Josie?" Then yelling toward the men saddling their horses, "You men can't leave, I need you for the chores around here."

"Guess you'll have to do them yourself, Lizzie." With a slap of my reins, I led the group back to Willow Lake. By the end of the day, we had built an acceptable corral attached to our large barn. I was thankful it had been finished the previous year. There would be some room for the boarded horses, but the barn was mainly used for the milking and stalls for the carriage horses.

Noticing the workers now seemed at a loss as to what was to happen to them now, I offered, "If you want to stick around, you can bed down in the barn loft tonight. Tomorrow we'll start building a bunkhouse and a proper shed for boarding the horses. I'll also need some pens for the two sows being delivered soon."

With any luck the weather would hold out to accomplish my goals. I planned to use the money from boarding the horses to pay my new workers. Hopefully George would chip in for building supplies. When he came home from Laketown, where he had opened his new law office, he brought me up to speed about his activities that day. "Elizabeth came to town and pleaded with the sheriff to block your actions. Then she stopped by my office and screamed at me that she would never sell now. You better hope the judge rules in your favor next month."

"Let's not quarrel. You know I hate it when we do. Let's just concentrate on getting through the next couple weeks."

That evening while sitting across from George at the dining table, I sketched out my first concept of the town I wanted to build at Willow Lake. Right now, it was just a dream, but someday I vowed to make it a reality. Even though George's office was now in Laketown, I didn't like the place. After living in both Momence and Rensselaer, Laketown always appeared to me to be an unproductive little burg. It just didn't have the potential to become a flourishing community. I showed the drawing to George.

"You are something, you know that? You're the only person I know who would want to build their own town."

That weekend, George and I held a reception for all the visitors coming from Chicago to board their horses. Some paid their groomers to take the horse tied at the back of a carriage to our homestead, and some came themselves to see where the horses would be boarded. I explained to each customer that conditions would be greatly improved when the horse stable was completed. Most were satisfied and paid in cash before they left. One disgruntled man decided to take his horse to a place in Momence instead.

The next week, a flurry of building activity continued. The shed for the horse corral went up quickly and the men then began on the bunkhouse. George had come through with money for the materials which the men transported from either Rensselaer or Momence. Many sawmills had popped up along the Kankakee because of the rich abundance of trees along the river, so supplies were not a problem.

On Sunday evening, George and I enjoyed a quiet meal at home and retired early to spend time in one another's arms. Our love making was slow and leisurely, enjoying each other's feelings. Afterward, George fell asleep in my arms, but my mind was on fire once again, thinking about all the things I wanted us to accomplish in the future.

When I woke the next morning George had moved away from me during the night. No sound came from his side of the bed. I felt for his hand. Cold!

"George, no!" Sobbing, I hugged him and kept repeating, "No, George. Why did you leave me?"

~

After a quick telegraph, Crawford came home to help me with the viewing and burial, but I insisted he return to his studies after a week at home. "George would have wanted you to get your law degree. I think he secretly wished you would join him in his law practice when you graduated."

"You sure you'll be, okay? I hate leaving you during this awful time."

I wasn't okay, but for his sake, I had to put on a brave face. I didn't want him to miss out on his schooling.

For a time, I suspended the building projects. I couldn't face the day-to-day business of the farm, spending most of the time in bed. But gradually, I realized there was no one else that could be in charge, and it would be up to me to move forward. I called Josiah into the house. "I'm ready to finish what we started. Do you think you could get the men organized again to finish the bunkhouse and build the fences for the hogs that will be arriving soon?"

"Yes, Ma'am. We've just been waiting for your word. They're anxious to work."

~

In March, I received notification to appear in the U. S. Circuit Court in Rensselaer for the hearing involving the parcels of land I truly felt belonged to me. Dressing in my best black mourning dress, I added a large black hat with a veil covering my face, even though I wasn't wearing mourning black any other time. Perhaps the outfit would make the judge more lenient to my plight. On the fourth Tuesday of the month, I drove myself to the hearing. When I entered the courtroom, many heads turned to look at my black attire. Just the response I had hoped for.

I needed no lawyer because George had filed all the necessary paperwork. When they called my case, Elizabeth stood at the opposite table with her attorney. He started with, "Your honor, this suit is unnecessary. My client's husband did not leave a will, so all property reverts to his widow, my client."

Judge Morrow looked down kindly as I dabbed my eyes with my black handkerchief. "I've had a chance to read over the proposal Mrs. Morris's late husband, George, wrote before he so suddenly passed away. Mrs. Morris is requesting the property adjacent to the original gift her father deeded to her, not all of Riley's Grove. This would square off her property and to me it seems she should be entitled to some of the acreage her father owned even though he was negligent in the writing of a will. I am ruling in favor of Mrs. Morris. She will pay the landholder one dollar, and also pay for any necessary survey costs."

I could feel Elizabeth's eyes staring at me, but I didn't reciprocate. "Thank you, Your Honor." I left the courthouse before I had to have any confrontation with Elizabeth.

Chapter 17

Bailey stood and gave her aunt a hug. "I'm so sorry you lost your dear husband. I can't imagine dealing with all that. I don't know what I'd do if something were to happen to John."

Josie sighed and wiped away a tear that had formed in her eye. "We weren't married that long, but George was the love of my life. My other two relationships were just practice for the real thing. After he died, my whole outlook changed, and I'm sad to say, not for the better. Maybe that's why people didn't like me very much. I was determined to make a success of my farm anyway I could. In pioneer days women were confined to the interior of the home, but I felt a woman should engage in whatever line of work she felt she could succeed. I chose the raising of pigs. Not every woman is mentally able to engage in the hog business, but the raising of pigs gave me the means to make my farm profitable and a practical means to develop my wealth."

"Ewww, I don't think I could raise pigs. Give me writing any day." Bailey screwed up her nose. Holding up her pages of notes, she continued. "I've got plenty of material here to write several articles. Do you mind if we take a break for a couple days?"

"That's fine. I'm getting a little tired of talking anyway." I'm going upstairs to take a nap.

Bailey worked the rest of the afternoon on her article. She wanted to show her aunt in a favorable light in what she wrote, but the comments she had received on previous stories were asking for more excitement. She needed to find a way to make the articles interesting but still true to the life of Josie Morris.

After the long 4th of July weekend, Bailey turned in the article that included the love story between her aunt and George. At breakfast on Monday she said, "I can't wait to see the comments I get from the tragic tale of your love story, Aunt Josie."

"You're such a romantic," teased John.

But Bailey's enthusiasm prompted Josie to ask if she wanted to hear more of her story. "I have to warn you, I'm afraid the next phase of my life, I get rather nasty to people. I guess I just soured on things after George was taken from me. A lot of what happened I now regret."

1898-1900

Determined to make a success of my business, I used my father's idea of dividing the farm into smaller units. Soon after all my building projects were completed, I used George's estate to pay for the surveyal of my property into individual farms of one hundred sixty or three hundred twenty-acre farms. Each farm was equipped with its own implements, horses and buildings. I provided seed and soon grains were under cultivation on about three-quarters of Willow Lake, and the balance of the land remained in blue-grass pastures, some with oak woodlands. My problem was finding enough honest, hardworking individuals who would be willing to work the land and share the profits with me.

On one of my trips to Momence, I heard of a family living on a houseboat near Shelby. They had traveled from the Brown Ranch near San Pierre where the father, James, had been working stacking hay. Nine family members, several dogs and a flock of chickens jammed themselves onto a thirty-four by fourteen-foot houseboat. They had reached Shelby but couldn't go further because workers were driving pilings for a new bridge. This sturdy family seemed exactly the kind I needed at Willow Lake. Before returning home, I drove to Shelby to find the father, James Hall. When I located the stranded houseboat, I called out, "Hello, there, anyone there?"

Several bodies poked their noses out, but a man called out, "Can I help you, lady?"

Eyeing this large, robust man, sporting a hearty smile, I felt reassured about sharing my idea. "I have a proposition for you, Mr. Hall. I think you might be interested."

Jim Hall and his family were just one of many that I enlisted to work my land, but Jim became more like a right-hand man. I put him in charge of the individual farms and their workers. I was never sorry I had stopped to talk to him that day. Later I heard the new bridge was finished at Shelby. I was thankful Jim, and his family had already decided to abandon their idea to continue on their trip on their houseboat.

Josiah, our first hired man, had also remained at Willow Lake, and he became the foreman in charge of most of the livestock. He and I made several trips to fill the place with an improved class of livestock, including a herd of milk cows and Aberdeen-Angus cattle. My starter herd of two spotted Poland-China hogs had grown into the best stock available in northwest Indiana.

Once most of the snow had thawed in the spring of 1901, Josiah and the other hired hands began the roundup. Just like when I was a teenager, I looked forward to this activity every spring and fall. Wearing my dungarees and flannel shirt with a large wide-brimmed hat to tame my hair, I rode along with the men.

One day on the trail, after doing some necessary business behind a large bush, walking my horse back toward the camp, I overheard a conversation that upset me terribly. The whispered voices made me stop and take in the exchange.

"That woman won't know how many animals she has that are supposed to be shipped. Cutting a few here and there out of the herd won't matter. She's got too many to sell there in Laketown anyway."

"I don't know. She and that Josiah fella, keep pretty good tabs on everything."

"You want to be a hired hand the rest of your life? We can sell off a few cows and get some cash to make a start on our own place. Tonight, we'll move a few cows back north to my rental."

"Okay, but let's not get greedy."

I recognized the voices as Jed Hopkins and his brother, Clyde, both farm renters, men with families. Josiah had hired both as extra help for the roundup. It saddened me to think these men would take the chance of losing their farmstead.

That night Josiah, myself and Jim, waited, horses saddled, for their thievery. With a shotgun at my side, once we spied their movement, we mounted up and trotted to catch up to the small raiding party. Opening fire with a warning shot into the air, when we caught up, I shouted, "Where do you think you're going with my cattle? Turn them around and go back to your homes. We don't need your thieving kind on this drive."

After George's death, sometimes my orders were not taken seriously by my employees, but after that night when word got around, I had appeared on the scene with a loaded shotgun, there was no doubt who was the boss. My inability to keep reliable hired help may have been attributed to my uncompromising attitude, but I didn't need dishonest men at my backdoor. I decided to give the Hopkins brothers a week to move on.

The next day, continuing with the roundup, the huge herd walked slowly ahead of Josiah and me, moving as unconcerned about their fate as a chicken pecking the ground before butchering for Sunday dinner.

"Miss Josie, we're getting too many animals for the stockyard in Laketown to handle. The Monon Line trains coming through can't hold all of the cattle to ship to the city. Some of the cattle need to stay too long in the pens and they start to lose weight."

That got me thinking, and in October I made another trip to Chicago to meet with the heads of the Chicago, Indiana, & Southern Railway. Crawford had drawn up papers showing the number of livestock I shipped out of Laketown each year. Another paper I brought proposed that I would transfer some of my land, four miles of right-of-way, one hundred feet wide if they would consider building their railway into the area of Willow Lake. I also promised to build a stone station on the line and showed them my drawings of a future town in that area. Through these negotiations the Chicago, Indiana, and Southern Railroad did indeed agree to build a new line right to the spot where I wanted to build my town. As soon as I returned to Willow Lake, we began building stockyards, eventually having the capacity to hold five thousand head of cattle, and the railroad sidings would save us from making the long trek to Laketown.

~

On my return from Chicago, after the incident of cattle rustling, I started a habit of patrolling my property to police the boundaries of my Willow Lake property most every late afternoon. The Shatner gold always remained in the back of my mind. I couldn't have trespassers, who might stumble onto the gold before me. Dressed in men's clothing and riding in my carriage, pulled by two horses, with a shotgun by my side, I felt a little like Anne Lister, a.k.a. 'Gentleman Jack,' who included men's accessories as part of her fashion.

One day I spied on some boys I did not recognize with buckets in hand. Stopping my team, I confronted the boys pointing my gun at them. "You're on private property. Let me see what you have in those buckets." To me, these boys represented the same type of thievery as the cattle rustlers and had to be dealt with sternly.

One of the boys came forward, his whole body shaking like a leaf in the wind, his words coming out in short, ragged gasps. "We didn't think you'd mind if we picked a few berries."

When he placed the buckets in front of me, I don't know what came over me, but I suppose I was still angry about the Hopkins brothers' betrayal. Without thinking it through, I quickly threw the berries on the ground and crushed them with my feet. "Now, stay away from my property."

I climbed back into my carriage and watched as they walked back in the direction of Laketown. The little devils must have hidden until I was gone. Driving into the entrance of my home, I saw smoke rising in the area where I had had the meeting with the boys.

Heading to the bunkhouse, I found Josiah standing outside already looking in the direction of the smoke. He ran to the carriage. "Move over Ma'am."

Josiah took the reins and driving like a mad man, we followed the smoky pillar. I could never prove it, but those boys must have returned and set fire to a forty-acre field of wheat which was ripe and ready to cut, a total loss.

Instead of blaming myself for treating them badly, I'm afraid I became more wary of folks and more disagreeable, trusting only those who I kept in my close circle. I became fiercely possessive and more aggressive and competitive toward outsiders. Because of my actions, people in Laketown snubbed me when I frequented the shops. I began to travel five miles out of my way to catch a train rather than taking the chance of running into some of the people in the town.

Chapter 18: 1905-1908

With the soon to be completed railroad to Willow Lake, I could now go ahead with my plans to build my model town. Ideas for the project swam around in my brain like schools of tiny fish, carried by the movement of the waves. I couldn't seem to settle into any sort of calm existence. To calm my nerves somewhat, each day I worked with my hired hands trying to complete the stockyard fencing before the next roundup and shipment.

No matter how hard I worked on the homestead, come nightfall, I always dressed for the evening meal. My housekeeper knew I expected dinner to be set in the dining room whether it was just me or a number of additional guests. Peeking into the kitchen before leaving the house, I called out, "Don't forget, I'm expecting a whole rabble of guests tonight for dinner, Molly. I'd like to impress them. I'm hoping to get their approval for a plan that I've drawn up, so I want to get them happily fed and maybe even a little drunk."

Wiping the flour from her hands onto her apron, Molly came to the foyer and handed me a wide slice of her homemade bread slathered with jam. "Don't you worry, Miss Josie. I know exactly how to get a person in a happy frame of mind. I'll be making roast venison with blackberry sauce, sweet potatoes and lots of other good dishes. Those folks won't know what hit them." Her melodious laugh resonated through the large foyer, and I knew the dinner would be lovely.

Leaving Molly to work her magic, I first went to the cellar to choose the wine for the evening's meal. Then my day began with first taking a quick ride around my property and next, heading to see how the fencing had progressed at the stockyard location. Men scattered and tried to look busy as I drove the horses into the worksite at a fast trot. Why was it that when the boss was not around, the work became slower?

"Let's get this corral done today, fellas, I got a group coming out from Laketown later today. I want them to see this so they can imagine for themselves the scope of what I plan to do here."

A week ago, the railroad workers had finished the line to Morris along with the spur to the stockyard. By fall we'd be ready to ship my cattle from Morris instead of taking them to Laketown. The less I had to deal with the people there, the better my life would be. The treatment I received while closing George's law office left a sour taste in my mouth for Laketown. I didn't care if I ever went back there. While shopping for some items at the local mercantile, I heard some chatter from two women in the next aisle.

"I see that Josie Morris is in town closing Mr. Morris' law office. Poor man. He was so nice. He helped us when we had some legal issues, you know."

The other voice added, "Seems hard to believe he just died naturally. They say she killed her first two husbands. I wouldn't doubt she had something to do with Mr. Morris's death, too."

"Oh my, do you really think so?"

"She's probably ready to move on to a new husband. That Josiah fella seems pretty friendly with her. He'll be moving into the big house with Josie before long, mark my words."

Grabbing my purchases, I hurried to the front to pay and rushed out to make my way back to George's office. Feeling his presence, the sobs racked by whole body. After a bit, I controlled my breathing and began the job of packing George's items into boxes. Hearing those nasty comments made me even more determined to make my town of Morris a success.

Shaking those thoughts from my head, I stepped down from my buggy, tied the horses to the corral, and started helping to carry fence posts from a pile delivered yesterday from the sawmill to the area where men dug holes to place each post into the ground. Other men would place the cross rails and nail them in place. Before long, with this consistent work, the corral had begun to shape up. Around noon, we took a break and the men who brought some jerky or hardtack sat in the shade to rest and eat.

After working another hour after lunch, I called out to Josiah, "I need to quit early today. Got those folks coming. You make sure these men keep at it until almost dark. We've got to get this done soon."

"I'll do my best, but some of these guys just don't seem like they want to work except if you're around." Josiah picked up another rail and walked back to the corner of the fence.

Driving my team back toward the house, my thoughts again circled around with the speed of the carriage wheels. I'd learned a lot in the past few years since George died, about running the farm. It had become clear that my vision wasn't always what the workers held dear. They needed monetary incentives to do the work, whereas I worked for the gratification it gave me. According to the Bible, we're only given threescore and ten, so I wanted to accomplish as much as possible each day. That's why this dinner was so important tonight. I needed to convince the county to give me permission to build my town, not only for my own benefit, but for my renters. Having a community of their own would give them a place of belonging.

Two carriages stood in front of the house when I pulled into the barnyard. Handing the reins to Lawence, the stable boy, I jumped down and hurried upstairs to change. With a quick washing, I stepped out of the pants I wore while working and tore off my shirt. Stepping into the high-neck, floor-length gown with a fitted bodice and a full, flowing skirt, suddenly I felt transformed from a hardened pioneer woman to an elegant lady. The intricate lace details, embroidery, and embellishments added a softness to my reflection that I wouldn't want to show to my guests. My persona needed to be that of an articulate and cultured lady, but also, I wanted to present a side of me where I could be independent and capable. Sweeping my hair up to pile it on my head and holding it there with a bejeweled comb, I felt ready to meet the men who held my fate in their hands.

My guests had gathered in the parlor according to Molly's directions. She had started them on glasses of wine and their voices were already quite forceful.

Nodding to the women, instead I joined the circle of men. "So happy you all could make it tonight. I'm sure you won't be disappointed."

The oldest of the four men, James Wood, raised his glass. "Mrs. Morris, I hope you won't keep us in suspense for long."

Smiling, I motioned toward the dining room. "Shall we go in to dinner? Molly has some wonderful dishes prepared for us."

As we entered the large room, I noticed the women taking note of the intricate moldings, the ornate wallpaper and the ceiling medallions. The beautifully set dining table, large enough to accommodate all my guests, featured curved lines and flowered upholstery, matching the emerald-green floor-length drapes.

While the dinner was served, my guests made their appreciation known to Molly for her skill in the kitchen. Her flushed face became even brighter red as they gushed over the dinner she had prepared. She could not keep from smiling when Mrs. Clemens asked for the recipe for the roast venison and the blackberry sauce. "I can write it out while you enjoy your coffee and lemon cake, Missus," chirped Molly.

During the table conversations, I kept attuned to the women's voices to see if any matched the ones I had heard in the mercantile. Thankfully none of these women were the culprits.

Toward the end of the meal, everyone gave James their attention when he raised his glass to make a toast. "To our wonderful hostess, thank you, Josie, for all you're doing here at Willow Lake."

A polite clapping followed, then James continued, "This areas' future depends on the channeling of the Kankakee River. Just last week, some of us got together and formed the Kankakee Reclamation Company." He turned to me, "I know this was a dream of your father's. Once we get that river tamed, the farming potential in this valley will soar." James had been around when my father worked so diligently to open the shelf in Momence, so he knew how much it meant to him.

"That's great news. I'm sure my father would have wanted to be part of that group if he was still here." I stopped for effect, looking around the table. "He would also want you to approve the plan that I want to share with you all tonight. It will also help with developing the Kankakee River area." I stood to take the rolled paper from the buffet top behind me. With dramatic flair, I pulled the ribbon bow and unrolled the drawing Crawford and I had so meticulously fashioned.

"Gentlemen and ladies, this is my vision for a new town, named Morris, after my late husband, George Morris. With your permission, I intend to build it as drawn. We already have the railroad in place that we needed." Pointing to the drawing, I went on, "You can see diagonal streets will meet at a central area which is set aside for a large park. The areas in between will be divided into lots for homes for the workers in the town. Eventually Morris will include a block plant, hotel, railway stations, a combination general store and post office, church, school, and cottages for employees."

My voice had risen as I talked and when I stopped, silence enveloped the table. From the shocked looks on the faces of my guests, my heart sank like a rock falling from a bridge. I gave them time to study the drawing before I pressed them for their thoughts. "I was hoping for an answer tonight. What are your thoughts?"

The men looked from one to another, then Richard Clemens spoke. "We'd like to have some time to discuss this. I'm afraid we can't give you an answer tonight. If it works for everyone, we'll come back tomorrow to see the stockyard. I hear it's almost finished." Heads nodded in agreement.

I tried not to show my disappointment as I grabbed the drawing from the table and rolled it. When my guests left, I hurried to my room to undress and crawled into the bed George and I had shared. I kept his dressing gown thrown across his pillow and tonight I held it close, breathing in, trying to inhale the little I had left of him. Before long, his scent would be gone, and I would be alone again with nothing to remind me of him.

Chapter 19: 1908

The next morning, I woke to the sounds of thunder and rain hitting the windowpanes. The lace inner curtains moved a miniscule measure each time the ferocious wind increased its onslaught on the outside of my bedroom. With these current weather conditions, I put off getting up. The stockyard would be a muddy mess, so, I snuggled back down under my sheet for another hour listening to the passing cacophony. Indiana summer storms typically blew themselves into a frensy and just as fast moved on to open up the afternoon with stifling heat and unbearable humidity.

Perhaps today would be different and the wind would blow in some cooler air into the stockyard along with my expected board members. My insides twisted thinking of the decision they'd have for me today. I needed their approval. Typical of my industrious nature, I had already ordered the Portland cement and hired a couple men who knew how to produce blocks. The block plant was positioned west of the railroad and south of my future town and soon the town's first building, a depot, would be erected out of this block. Just thinking about all my future plans made me feel giddy to get started.

After dozing in and out for about another half hour, the next time I took stock; the winds had died down and only a soft pitter patter from the diminishing drops were hitting the panes. Getting up now seemed a necessity as the day ahead loomed larger than a year of holidays.

Molly was already busy setting breakfast out on the buffet when I entered the dining room. "Sorry, I can't eat much this morning, Molly. Just a boiled egg and some of your wonderful bread will do me. I've got to get out to the stockyard site early to make sure we're ready for our visitors. Who knows when they'll show up."

Molly began packing up the extra food she had laid out. "The way they ate and drank last night, I don't think they'll be around till later today. Especially with this storm that came through."

With the way the day's weather had started, very few of my workers had arrived at the site, but as the skies cleared, more of the crew showed up. By noon, the work had progressed well, but the scorching sun forced me under a tree to sit and try to get a little relief.

Josiah joined me. "Almost finished. With any luck, we might get the last of it done today. What's our next project? I know you've got lots of plans circling around in that head of yours."

"In a few weeks, we'll have to start rounding up the cattle for shipment. What an exciting time that will be. This will be the first time we'll ship from our own stockyard. But the rest depends on the decision I get today from the county board. They're supposed to be here sometime today. It may not be until late, though, after the partying they did last night."

As I expected, it wasn't until late that afternoon when I heard the faint sound of a carriage coming our way. Peeking out from below my large-brimmed hat, a tornado swirled inside my chest at the site of the entourage heading our way. Not one but three carriages, full of men and women, no doubt all wanting to see the site for themselves so they could report back to their nosy friends in Laketown.

"Hi there, Mrs. Morris," said Jed Shipley, the first to pull to a stop in front of me.

I walked toward all three of the arriving carriages and when stopped I called out, "Hello, there everyone. I didn't expect such a large group, but welcome."

Waiting during the awkward time it took for the spectators to disembark; I brushed the mud from my lower pant legs and repositioned my hair under my hat. "If you'll follow me, you can get a better look at our nearly completed stockyard."

I led the group to the corrals near their carriages and let them see our work without any comment from me, listening as they talked to one another about the project. After viewing the stockyard fencing, I motioned for the group to once again follow. We walked about a quarter mile and stopped where a large grove of oak trees provided an abundance of shade for the group. "You're standing right in the middle of the park that will be set aside for the residents of my future town, Morris. What do you say? Won't this be a grand place for a park?"

From the looks on their faces, I was sure they didn't share my enthusiasm. My heart sank when James Wood spoke for the first time. "Josie, we know how much you want this, but really, do we need another town so close to Laketown?"

Grasping for anything that might sway their opinion, my hogs became my means to my end. "You know I'm raising hogs and plan on expanding my herd. If you approve the town of Morris, the people of Laketown won't have to put up with me shipping hogs their way. Some people don't like the smell of pigs. I just can't imagine why."

That got a chuckle from the group. Even James cracked a slight smile. He looked around the group and received nods from the other men. "We may as well give our blessing. You'd probably go ahead with it anyway. Go ahead and build your town, Josie."

My face broke into a huge smile. Without commenting on James' last words, I thanked the group, knowing full well, they thought me to be crazy and probably doubted whether I could accomplish my goal of a new town, anyway. Giving their permission was probably their way of letting me go ahead and fail, but they didn't know how tenacious I could be.

After delivering the good news to Josiah, I returned home. Plans were made to travel to Rensselaer the following day to meet with the surveyor I had hired. I hoped he would arrive within the next few days to lay out the streets for Morris according to my design. Prospects for the future town appeared promising, and I felt more optimistic than I had for a long while.

The fall months involved the round up and the shipping of cattle from Morris for the first time. After the block plant and depot were completed, the next project became the Morris Hotel, which was located east of the depot on Brevoort St. It was a two-story wood-frame building with eighteen rooms. The first floor contained an office, dining room, large kitchen, a small parlor and other rooms, with the sleeping rooms on the upper floor. Work slowed considerably in the winter months, but in the spring, the post office and the general store, a two-story block building, were constructed. The post office, located at the south end of the building, contained about thirty boxes for the people to come on their horses or buggies and pick up their mail. Adam Press had plans for opening a blacksmith's shop and eventually I'd add a church and school. My dream of the town of Morris was becoming a reality.

While Morris was shaping up to be a first-rate town, my relations with the people of Laketown and the surrounding area continued to be troublesome. A lot of it came about because of my stubborn nature. I had a hard time in those days admitting I might be wrong.

In the fall of 1909, I had contracted with Thomas Clayden to pick the corn in several of my fields. On one of my daily carriage rides around my property, I noticed cows grazing in one of the fields where he had picked my corn.

Driving like a crazed chariot driver, I found Josiah. "I need you to help me," was all I yelled and took off back for the field. When we got to the plot, Josiah pulled up beside me.

Getting out of the carriage and walking toward the cows, I nearly yelled my orders to Josiah. "I want those cows out of there and into a corral. Thomas didn't ask if he could pasture those animals in my corn."

"Now, Josie, those cows aren't hurting anything. Thomas picked most of the corn and they're just cleaning up the rest."

"That's not the point. He didn't ask permission. Get them locked up."

Josiah stared at me for a time, then got back on his horse and began to herd the cows toward the nearest corral.

After several days, When Thomas heard what I had done, he came to Willow Lake to confront me. "Just let them loose so I can take them back to my farm."

"They're mine now. You left them for me in MY field."

"At least let me water them. They're going to die of thirst if you let this go on."

Again, I felt I had to show I could be tough and uncompromising, so I declined to allow Thomas to take his cattle or water them. Another day passed, and Thomas returned with the constable from Laketown.

"Mrs. Morris, we have a warrant for you to appear in court at Rensselaer on Tuesday next week along with an order from the judge to turn loose the cows in question. If you don't comply, I'll be arresting you for cattle rustling."

That got to me. I was no cattle rustler, and I didn't want my Chicago contacts to pull their support for my town if they heard I had been convicted of rustling cattle. I never liked backing down, but this situation had gone too far. Getting locked up was not an option for me.

I smiled at the sheriff and flipped my long hair back behind my ear. "If I let Thomas have his cows and appear in court on Tuesday, do you think we could keep this out of the Chicago newspapers and settle this soon?"

They agreed to keep the situation local.

On the day I needed to appear in court, no longer able to dress in mourning attire to obtain the judge's sympathy, I wore a dark blue dress that complimented my blue eyes and auburn hair. The fitted bodice and A-line skirt whose hem consisted of a wide plain ruffle; gave the impression of a professional, sophisticated working woman whose only intention was to benefit others. When I walked into the courtroom, I wanted no one to picture a vengeful woman who could treat an animal poorly.

As I took my seat, I could feel the eyes of the courtroom on me. The trial proceeded with Thomas giving his testimony with the judge, a stern-looking man, listening intently.

When it was my turn to speak, I said, "Your honor, I'm no cattle rustler. I was merely protecting my property. Thomas ran his cows on my land without my permission, and I had no choice but to confine them. I regret my decision to withhold water from the animals."

Josiah had accompanied me thinking he would also be called upon to testify, but it seemed as if the judge had heard enough. I was happy Josiah didn't have to add what he remembered of the day because I didn't want him to lie for me under oath.

The judge raised an eyebrow while deliberating for a moment. "Mrs. Morris, I find you guilty of mistreatment of animals but not of cattle rustling. You will be fined heavily for your actions."

I nodded, accepting the judgment, but secretly feeling as if I had won. After the gavel came down, I left the courtroom without speaking to anyone, smiling to myself.

Chapter 20

Josie watched her niece as she scribbled some more notes from today's sharing. "I told you; you wouldn't like the person I was during this part of my life. In the last few years, I've had a chance to reflect and it's no wonder people think of me as a grumpy old lady. I really was a stinker at times after my dear George was gone. It was as if I was upset with the whole world."

Bailey didn't like hearing about Aunt Josie's mean streak, but she had agreed to write the whole story, not just the good parts. "It can't get any worse, can it?"

Josie looked down at her hands. She knew there was more nastiness ahead.

1916-1917

Morris became a bustling place. Besides trying to complete the town's business establishments, the town's residents also worked building their homes. Each of the planned streets contained several houses, laid out opposite one another. Thankfully most of the work had been completed before the start of the war in April of 1917. President Woodrow Wilson signed a resolution formally declaring war against the Imperial German Government. Because so many young men had decided to enlist, the meager crews at both the homestead and at Morris, made work difficult and slow to accomplish.

Although staying connected to all the activities in Morris kept me busy, my main concern remained breeding my Poland China hogs. No other aspect of my life received more attention because my pigs provided the practical means of making my farm pay. At every chance I got, I would be there when the sows farrowed, recording the size of the litter and keeping meticulous records necessary for improving the stock. We culled the runts and kept the best and biggest boars and sows for breeding. Looking past the smell of breeding hogs, I focused on the capital to be gained.

Each year I attended the International Livestock Exposition in Chicago. The extravagance of staying at the Atlantic Hotel became the highlight of my year. Walking into the vast high-ceilinged entrance, guests were welcomed at the center of the lobby by red and green armchairs placed evenly around a huge colorful area rug. My usual second-floor room looked down on the lobby through French doors which opened onto a narrow balcony.

After the porter accompanied me to my room with my luggage and I settled in, I took my evening meal in the Winter Garden. The many live plants and garden-painted walls made me feel as if I was back home in the Kankakee Marsh. Breakfast was also a treat in this dining room because of the skylit ceiling. The rising sun moved across the ceiling as it rose from the east. I loved these city interludes into my life, but I also looked forward to being back in the marsh. Eating in this lush garden room kept me from getting too homesick.

Many of the other attendees at the Livestock Exposition also stayed at the Atlantic and I made many beneficial contacts when we retired to the bar after dinner. During the year I continued to correspond with many of the breeders I met at the exposition.

On one of my trips to Chicago, I met an interesting couple who had been married for only twelve hours. With the bar nearly empty because of the war effort, the wife, Mattie, asked if they could join me for a drink. Her high-pitched laughter soon got on my nerves, but I also felt bad for her. Her husband, Winfred, a rancher from Oregon, couldn't keep his eyes from roaming toward my chest.

In a pompous voice, Winfred explained, "I needed a wife, so I placed an ad in a farming magazine, and Mattie was the lucky one who answered."

After a couple more drinks, Winfred, getting louder with each, excused himself for a short time. As soon as he left, Mattie grabbed my arm. "I don't know what to do. I'm afraid I've been duped. He married me simply on account of my money, I'm sure. He already borrowed eight hundred eighty dollars."

"Perhaps you should inform the police." While saying this,

Winfred joined us back at the table. His eyes opened wide at the word, police. Taking Mattie's hand, he pulled her up and the two left me alone to wonder what would become of this ill-fated marriage. I knew from experience, the wrong match could be deadly, but how wonderful the right combination could be. I felt grateful I had ended my relationships with such a caring partner such as a man like George.

Later that evening I heard such a ruckus out in the lobby, I dressed again enough to join the group that had congregated there. When I made it down the stairs, someone said a thinly clad woman had jumped out of the first-floor room into the bushes, while calling for a 'copper,' only badly scraping her ankles.

I ran out to the street; sure it was Mattie who had jumped. When she saw me approach, she hobbled to
me, weeping, waving a handful of cash and stocks she said were worth about ten thousand dollars. I held her until the policeman escorted her away to the station house.

Winfred yelled after them. "She must be temporarily demented."

The next morning, I went to the police station, but Mattie had been released to her husband. Hoping I could help Mattie, I asked back at the hotel for their room number, but the clerk said they had already checked out.

The incident made me cynical and convinced me that trusting people was usually a mistake. I became more determined to do things independently. Poor Mattie wouldn't have that luxury. It's no wonder so many women were joining the National American Woman Suffrage Association. Women felt they deserved the same rights as men had. Maybe I'd check into joining while I was in Chicago.

But first, meeting with Crawford for lunch would lift my spirits. He now worked for one of George's classmates whose law practice flourished in the busy downtown area of Chicago.

Crawford insisted on having me meet him at the Walnut Room in Macy's, the first-ever restaurant to open inside a department store. The sophisticated, classy atmosphere matched the reason Crawford wanted me to meet him there. Sitting with him at the table when I entered the dining area, was a beautiful blond woman, dressed in the latest style with a fashionable feather-clad hat on her head.

Crawford rose to give me a peck on the cheek. "Mom, I want

you to meet my fiancé, Elaine Dutton."

My face must have shown the shock I experienced because both young people laughed at my momentary loss of words. "I'm so happy Crawford has finally found someone, Elaine. I was beginning to wonder if he would ever settle down and marry."

After giving Elaine a huge hug, I wiped away the tears that had formed in my eyes. "I've been so worried he would be called for duty for this blasted war, even at his age. Perhaps now, we won't have to worry about that."

We had a delightful lunch during which I had the opportunity to become acquainted with my future daughter-in-law. She was not only beautiful but articulate, well-educated and fun to be with. It didn't hurt either that she was the daughter of one of the lawyers Crawford worked for.

"Let's do something more to celebrate." said Crawford. "I saw in the paper, there's going to be an air show out by the lake today. You'd like to see that, wouldn't you, Mom? It's such a nice day and we could sit on the beach to watch. Let's go get a taxi."

Elaine smiled and shook her head, yes. His excitement spread to me also, so we paid our bill and hailed a taxi for the lakefront. A huge crowd filled the beaches for the Aero Meet being held in Grant Park. Crawford purchased a blanket from a passing vendor, and we made ourselves comfortable on the beach to watch the aviators perform their tricks. However, our celebration ended in tragedy. Mike Badger of Pittsburgh, flying a Baldwin biplane, executed a low-level flyover of Grant Park, ending with a dramatic climb. We watched in horror as his plane tore apart. It fell fifty feet, and we heard later the wealthy daredevil died at St. Luke's Hospital.

As soon as we could navigate through the spectators, Crawford rushed us out of the park, trying to salvage the celebratory mood we had experienced just an hour previous. Stunned, we couldn't get the sight of the plane falling to the ground out of our minds. I was glad they offered to accompany me back to my room at The Atlantic Hotel. Our taxi ride transpired in near silence.

Once in my hotel room, I flopped down on the nearest chair and tried to persuade Crawford and Elaine that I would be fine. "I've had way too much excitement today and I'm exhausted. Don't worry about me. I'm going to bed and tomorrow I'll be catching the train back to Kankakee, then back to the safety of Willow Lake."

After we said good-bye with hugs and kisses, I picked up the complimentary newspaper left on the table in my room. Apparently, another pilot died in the same air show. The Chicago Daily Tribune stated "St. Croix Johnstone, flying a Moisant monoplane, died as his plane fell into Lake Michigan about a mile offshore, opposite Twelfth Street. He was attempting to do a corkscrew maneuver when eight hundred feet above the lake, the spidery monoplane tipped a bit, shot downward with a sickening swoop, overturning just before it splashed in the water." I was so happy we got away from there when we did.

As the air show tragedy lingered in my thoughts, I found it hard to fall asleep. The night was alive with the city's sounds, and my mind kept replaying the horrifying sight of the plane's descent. I awoke the next morning with the events of the previous day still casting a shadow over me, not feeling a bit rested.

Determined to regain a sense of normalcy, I packed my belongings and checked out of the hotel, the weight of the experience pressing heavily on my shoulders. As I boarded the train back to Kankakee, I hoped the familiar surroundings of Willow Lake would bring me solace, as it usually did. The war in Europe had everyone on edge, so people kept to themselves on the train. The solitary ride suited me fine.

Sitting by the train's window, I watched the landscape change from the urban sprawl to the serene countryside. The rhythmic clatter of the train wheels was somewhat soothing, and I allowed myself to drift into thoughts of home. Willow Lake had always been a sanctuary, a place where I could find peace and clarity and soon, I would feel that again.

Reflecting on all the recent events, I realized how unpredictable and fragile life could be, but it was also full of positive moments. Though the memory of the air show accident would stay with me, I chose to focus on the joyous moment of meeting Elaine, the laughter we shared, and the bond we formed. I looked forward to the wedding they were planning for October.

Chapter 21: 1917

My train ride home first took me back to Kankakee where I had stabled my horses and carriage. I desperately needed sustenance since all meals on trains had been suspended because of supply shortages. Knowing the trip to Willow Lake to be another trek without food, before going to claim my transport, I walked across the street from the depot to grab a quick bite to eat at the café. After ordering, I couldn't help but overhear the tableful of men near me who were discussing the most recent news about the dredging of the Kankakee.

One of the men expounded. "Won't be long now for that big dredge to get close to Shelby. I went to see it the other day. Looking back upstream, the river is as straight as an arrow now, just a big ditch."

"I don't know. The farmers all want it straightened so they have more farmland, but it sure is going to change things around here." The speaker shook his head in disbelief.

I listened with mounting interest. As I ate and listened to more of their conversation, I made up my mind to go see this dredge they talked about. Before I drove back to Willow Lake, I would take a slight detour to see the ditching operation. When else could I see history being made in the way my father had envisioned?

I arrived on the east side of Shelby, and followed a winding path towards the river as far as I could get my team to travel without getting stuck in the mud. Tying the horses to a low branch, I trudged through the bayou to see if I could catch a glimpse of the dredging operation. Coming to a slight clearing, the huge machine appeared to the right of me like a leviathan from the deep, moving slowly towards the west sitting right in the middle of all that water.

The digging was done in one operation, and the result was a ditch behind the dredge as wide as the cut it made. Digging up a shovel-full on one side, the machine would throw it all up and make a bank. The next swipe, they'd throw it on the other side to add to the bank there. The dredge floated right in the water and everything they needed was right on the dredge so if anything broke, they could fix it right there. It looked as if about a half a dozen men worked on the dredge including firemen and blacksmiths.

Tears stung my eyes as I remembered this had been my father's dream to see the Kankakee converted from a meandering, two hundred fifty-mile-long waterway to a series of canal-like, straight-line ditches so more land could be productive. I watched for about an hour not wanting to miss the action, but the sun moving to the west along with the dredge meant I had to get going.

As I drove my team the last few miles to my home at Willow Lake, my eyes surveyed the woodland areas along either side of the road, fenced to make the sections hog tight. In late summer to early fall, the hogs grazed in these spaces, feeding on bluegrass and acorns for two months, along with the properly balanced ration in the self-feeders. My heart swelled at thinking of how these pigs had changed my life. All because George suggested getting into raising hogs. If things continued to improve, I would soon be the largest breeder of Spotted Poland-China hogs in the nation. While at the International Livestock Exposition, I was honored for my breeding practices.

If only the government would quit interfering in the marketing of our livestock. For the good of the military, they urged people to forgo wheat, which was needed to bake bread for the AEF, and use cornmeal instead. This had caused the price of cornmeal, the traditional feed used for hogs, to triple. Many farmers feared losing money, so they cut back their production. I had plunged in deeper, hoping to reap bigger profits by using the government sponsored low-interest loans.

My head spun, thinking about all my financial issues. Would I ever be able to pay back the loans and get out of debt? Thinking about it made my stomach clench into knots. But right now, I needed a meal, a wash and my bed. In the morning, I would walk the woods and proceed with a better check on my hogs.

~

Early the next morning, taking my shotgun from the shelf, and making a beeline for the barn, I thanked Lawence for having my carriage ready to go again. He had fed, watered and brushed the horses last night. The boy was a marvel at his work. I reminded myself to add a little extra to his pay the following week.

Driving straight to the hog pastures, I parked and disembarked. The ground was soft from a recent rain and my boots sunk into the mud the hogs had disturbed with their snouts. I followed the walking path at the ridge checking for any hogs that were in distress for some reason. Head down, watching where to place my feet to keep from sinking too far into the mud, I stopped short. Something very shiny protruded from the ground. Using a strong stick, I poked around the area, being careful not to bury the item again, and as I stirred the dirt, a couple more shiny objects surfaced. Could it be? Had my hogs unearthed Shatner's gold? In my excitement I didn't check the area for workers and bent over to pick one up.

"Hi, Miss Josie. I thought I saw you roaming around out here. Glad to see you got back safely from Chicago." Josiah walked closer and I used the toe of my boot to cover the area with dirt while slipping the gold coin I had picked up into my jacket pocket.

Josiah continued to hover around so I couldn't retrieve any more of the coins. As we talked, I took note of exactly where we stood in the woods. Just before walking together back to my carriage, I dropped my lace trimmed hanky, hoping the hogs would not root in the area until I had a chance to return. With any luck at all, the hanky would still be there to mark the spot when I drove by later.

"How did things go in Chicago?" Josiah asked as he helped me up into the buggy. He always acted like a gentleman around me. If I hadn't sworn off men, he could have been a viable future partner. But George still filled my heart, and staying single seemed like a better choice for the success of my business. Besides, now that I found the gold, I wouldn't be sure if any suitor would be wanting me or my money.

While trying to answer Josiah's question, I got so nervous, it felt like a wadded-up sock got stuck in my throat. The excitement of finally finding Shatner's gold made my insides as wild as a mustang. "Oh, Josiah, could I tell you about it another time? I need to check one of the sows. I think she's ready to farrow."

Heading toward the farrowing shed, I watched as Josiah rode toward the stockyard. I grabbed a shovel from the corner of the shed, then waited until Josiah turned the corner. I hurried back into my carriage, pulled on the reins and drove my team back to the site of the coins. Walking toward the spot where I had found the first coin, my arms trembled as I clutched the shovel. Spotting my white hanky, I began to dig around, careful not to disturb what might be the nail keg, probably rotten years ago. But to my disappointment, only five gold coins lay below the surface of the dirt. Frantic, I dug deeper until I realized this was not the site of Shatner's gold. The five coins had been too close to the surface. Could it be, old Shatner had dropped these coins on the way to burying the rest? That had to be the explanation.

Not knowing how much the coins were worth or what to do with them, with trembling fingers, I hid them in my bureau drawer in a locking jewelry box Crawford had given me for my birthday last year. I tried to forget about the coins until I could get them appraised and decide how to deal with them. At this point, I no longer needed the money, so there was no big hurry.

In October, Crawford and Elaine's wedding was held at The Cathedral of the Holy Name because Elaine's family was Catholic. I attended the wedding but felt a little like an ugly duckling amid all the gorgeous swans. The elegantly adorned church made my own church, called the Mission of Morris, a tiny offering in comparison. It was of Presbyterian origin, but sometimes the minister took a head count and directed his sermon to the denomination that had the greatest number in attendance. The difference in churches, struck me as something God might frown on.

Elaine's brother, who was overseas fighting in the war, put a slight damper on the occasion, but regardless, Crawford and Elaine completed their nuptials. I only stayed until the wedding festivities ended and returned home the following day because we were in the middle of shipping cattle,

~

Traveling again to Chicago for a longer visit in an almost empty train car, I planned to spend the holidays with Crawford and Elaine. Before leaving, I had stitched the five gold coins inside the hem of my coat. Not only would I spend time with Crawford and Elaine, but I also intended to find a reputable coin dealer while in Chicago.

The day after Christmas I couldn't contain my excitement. "I'm making a trip downtown today to do a little shopping."

"Take Elaine with you, Mom. She loves to shop, and you can

get better acquainted."

Now what was I to do? I didn't want to hurt Elaine's feelings, but I really didn't want her to accompany me. Nature intervened. Elaine came down for breakfast and after trying to eat some oatmeal, she ran for the lavatory. I looked at Crawford, smiling. "I think that girl might be pregnant."

The look on Crawford's face was priceless. I stood to prepare to leave for my day of shopping. "Go to her, dear. She needs to know you're happy she's having your baby."

During my taxi ride downtown, I worked one of the coins out of the hem of my coat. They were all identical so one would be all I needed. When I arrived at the store, I asked the taxi driver to wait, assuring him it wouldn't take long. I had picked this store because the name, Anderson & Sons, sounded affluent and it was located in a upscale shopping area of Chicago.

The building was filled with displays and charts all dealing with the buying and selling of coins and other collectibles. Coins of all shapes and sizes filled the display cases. The musty smell of some of the displays made my breathing difficult. The quicker I could get an answer, the better.

A young clerk walked toward me. "Can I help you Ma'am?"

"Is your father here? I have a coin that I doubt if you would know much about." He looked crushed but I had to deal with someone who knew about old coins. Walking to the back of the store, he called out for his father. I followed him to the back counter hoping it would be more private.

An older gentleman with white hair that seemed to fly everywhere in an uncontrolled mess, came out of the back. He shoved his glasses up on his nose and leaned onto the counter. "How may I be of service, Ma'am?"

Digging the coin from my velvet bag, I placed it in front of him on the counter. He must have been used to all types of coinage because he showed no surprise. After adjusting his wire-rimmed glasses again, he picked up the coin to examine it.

"I'd like to know how much it's worth."

He placed the coin on a small scale, then removed it and bit down on the edge. Next, he held a magnet near the coin. After several minutes, in a heavily accented Italian voice he gave me his answer. "I can give you what its value is by weight, but the gold market is not good right now and with the war going on, collectors aren't buying much now either. I can give you twenty dollars for it."

I picked up my coin and deposited it back into my bag. "I'm sure you know. That's a twenty-dollar Double Eagle from 1855. I'm not in need of money that badly to sell it for face value." I held my head high and strolled out of his establishment.

Chapter 22: Spring to Late Summer 1918

Once back home at Willow Lake, I again placed the gold coins into the locked box and hid them in the back of my bureau drawer. Since they weren't worth what I had expected, I tried to put them far away in my memory. I needed to concentrate on improving my town and livestock rather than worrying about that darn gold. But just like a bad penny always turning up, those gold coins would creep back into my thoughts even though I tried to forget about them.

When the weather allowed, I began patrolling my property again. With my gun always ready, I'd drive my buggy watching for unwelcome animals and humans. Since finding the gold coins, I worried even more that someone would stumble onto the treasure before I would. Because of the war shortages, people had become more aggressive in trying to support their families with wild game and I didn't want poachers and trespassers roaming around where my livestock grazed.

In early spring, not anticipating trouble, I made my usual drive around my property. When I drove to the south side of the Willow Lake property, where a few swampy areas persisted, shots rang out, too close to be on the other side of my property line. Slowing the horse to a saunter and stopping thirty feet from the make-shift duck blind, I climbed down, and I ambled closer. I recognized the shooter as John Nottings, a resident of Laketown, who had been one of my guests the night I requested permission for the town of Morris. John owned a small farm near Laketown, but he often came to Morris for supplies, and he and his family attended the Morris church.

I called out to him. "Having any luck, John?"

Getting up from his reclining position behind the reeds, John turned and for a moment pointed his gun at me. Seeing it was me, he dropped the weapon to his side. "Got a couple so far, but I just got here. Sure are a lot of ducks this time of year. Didn't think you'd mind if I shot a couple so far from your house. With the war on, any extra meat we can get, helps."

"You know you're on my property, then?" With John's gun now at his side, I grabbed mine and aimed it at him. "I can't allow poachers, John. If I let you get by with it, everyone will think they can come out here to hunt."

"Don't get crazy, Josie. I'll move on."

"You can keep what you shot. I don't want your family to go hungry, but make sure you let everyone know, I won't tolerate trespassers on my land."

I kept my gun aiming his way as he walked toward his horse.

"Mark my words, Josie. Someday you'll be sorry for your ungenerous attitude." John mounted and rode away.

A year before I caught John on my property, he had purchased one of my China Poland sows. Josiah heard from John that the pig had died after birthing fifteen little piglets. They had managed to save most of them with bottle feeding.

"I got the idea he thought you knew the sow was sick when you sold it to him, Miss Josie." Josiah rubbed his hand through his thick beard and shook his head. "I don't like people talking bad about you."

"Don't worry. I'll deal with him, Josiah."

The evening after Josiah and I talked, before I even checked to see if what he had reported was true, I wrote a post to John informing him that I would no longer allow him to ship his hogs from the Morris depot if he continued to tell people that I had sold him damaged property. Hoping that this would end the feud, the next morning, I went to Morris for the church service, knowing I would probably see John and his family there.

The congregation had planned a carry-in lunch for after the service and Molly made a blueberry pie for me to bring. John and his wife Mary, and their four children also stayed for the social. Their circle of friends joined them, and the group seemed to have such camaraderie. With all my successes, most of my friends were business associates and I missed the kind of relationships this group enjoyed. Jealousy and the nasty disagreements between myself and John bubbled up inside and overcame me. I had just heard a beautiful message on the love that Jesus wants us to show to others, but I found myself unable to stop my slanderous comment about John to those sitting close to me.

I nearly shouted so those at John's table could hear as well. "I wonder where John Nottings got so many China Poland hogs and Aberdeen Angus cattle. His herd has gained more rapidly than by the usual means of breeding, farrowing and birthing, it seems. In the meantime, I've notice some of my stock is missing."

No one near me said a word for quite some time after my accusation. John stared my way, but didn't comment. He was a kind, generous person, and would not return my slander while sitting within the church. Thinking this would be the last of it. I went back to my business and didn't think about the incident again for several days. However, the next week, the constable from Rensselaer drove over to Willow Lake with a summons for me to appear in court the following week. I had forgotten about John's brother-in-law, Milton Graves, who just happened to be a lawyer. Together they sued me for slander. Again, I needed to appear in court.

On the day of the court appearance in Rensselaer, I dressed in my best plain dress and sensible shoes. Rolling my hair on top of my head, I looked like an old housewife as I stood before the court. The look was shocking to many, as lately most of my acquaintances only saw me in men's pants and flannel shirts. But this time my appearance didn't convince the judge of my innocence.

This lawsuit drew very few spectators, except those who were directly involved. Because of the small number of individuals in the courtroom, the dark-wood trim echoed as I walked to take my place at the front table. John Nottings nodded to me as I took my seat.

Jean Prosser, who sat to my right when I made the comment at the church social was first to testify, saying, "We all got the idea from what Josie said that she thought John had stolen her hogs and cattle."

Milton asked, "And what did Mrs. Morris say exactly?"

"She said she wondered where John had gotten so many Poland-China hogs and Aberdeen Angus cattle and that her livestock seemed to be dwindling."

The few spectators in the courtroom murmured and Judge Rynholt hit his gavel louder than necessary for order. Milton walked up to the judge. "I can produce at least three more witnesses who will testify to the same thing that Mrs. Prosser said. You also have before you the bill of sales for the cattle and pigs my client, John Nottings, bought. Do you want me to go on?"

The Judge studied the paperwork. "I have all I need to make a ruling. Mrs. Morris, I am ordering you to pay five hundred dollars to Mr. John Nottings and along with the payment, you will give him an oral and written apology."

I hurried from the courtroom, anxious to get away from all the nasty stares. Why had I said those things? George would have been so upset with me if he had lived to see my actions. However, if George had lived, I doubted I would have behaved so badly. It seemed I was just mad at the whole world most of the time. I needed to try to be a better person.

Before I could change my ways, the news I received when I arrived at Willow Lake, made me question whether God was punishing me for being so mean and nasty. "There's a telegram for you from Crawford in the drawing room on the table, Miss Josie." Molly's red eyes indicated she had already read the message.

She followed me into the room, sure I would need support. The last few years we had become friends rather than employer and employee. She put her arm around my shoulder as I read the telegram.

ELAINE LOST THE BABY. – STOP - VERY SICK WITH THE FLU – STOP -

DON'T COME – STOP - DON'T WANT YOU SICK ALSO – STOP -

I turned to Molly's shoulder, shocked at first, then began to sob uncontrollably. She held me until I could move without collapsing. She stirred me to the settee, and we sat together in front of the fire, each with our own thoughts until the fire died down. Every so often she would take my hand or I hers and share a few words of comfort. Even if I was feeling God's punishing hand, He also knew I would need a friend like Molly.

~

Bailey wiped the tears from her eyes and got up to hug her aunt. Josie sat like an uncompromising statue, but Bailey persisted. "How awful that Elaine lost her baby because of that flu. Wasn't there any medicine they could have given her?"

Josie patted Bailey's back. "Come now, it was a long time ago.

I did all the mourning I could back then." Josie sighed and Bailey pulled away to retrieve a hanky from her pocket.

"Actually, losing the baby was not all of the story. In September, Elaine succumbed to the disease, as well."

Bailey sat down, afraid her legs wouldn't hold her, unable to believe the heartache her aunt had experienced. "How could you and Crawford ever go on after that?"

"Keeping busy was the best medicine and we both did that, each in our own way."

Chapter 23: 1918

Of course, I ignored all warnings against traveling to Chicago but made my way there by automobile rather than by train. My friends, Steven and Patsy, in Kankakee, had purchased a contraption called a Model T. The last time I stopped to see them, Steven had insisted I go for a ride with them. After a nerve-wracking ride, I told him, "Give me my horses any day."

However, now I needed to eat my words. The automobile would be the best way to avoid contact with people as much as possible. I telegrammed my friends to explain my wish to go to Chicago for Elaine's funeral. Steven jumped at the chance to drive me.

On the morning before the scheduled funeral service, all valises packed, the automobile needed several steps to convince it to start. Steven's son manned the crank while he sat behind the wheel to quickly adjust certain knobs and buttons. Horses were still my choice, but having the luxury of this new way to travel would also keep me safer from the flu and not require stabling horses when we arrived. Luckily the dry weather in September made the marsh roads passable for the trip and we arrived at Crawford's home by midafternoon.

The Chicago Commissioner of Health had ruled that all funerals be limited to ten people, so the next morning, Elaine's priest came to the house to perform the service with only a small group gathered around the mandatory closed casket in Crawford's large parlor.

Everyone left as soon as the service was over, hurrying to their homes, hoping they wouldn't be detained by the Chicago police for coughing without using a handkerchief.

Steven and Patsy said their goodbyes and went out to prime the Model T for our journey home. I hugged Crawford as I prepared to leave. "Come to Willow Lake for a visit until all this flu is gone.

You've endured so much. You need a rest and enjoying the country air will help."

"I'll think about it. Maybe I'll see if my friend, Samuel, wants to join me. We could do some deer hunting."

"That's a wonderful idea. Hope to see you both soon." I gave him another hug, holding him as close as we dared.

As we drove from the city, the streets were quite empty and places like theaters and pool halls displayed signs stating, "Closed Because of Spanish Flu." I prayed for escape from the flu for all of us who had attended the funeral.

~

To my surprise, the first week of October, Crawford took me up on my invitation. He and his friend, Samuel, pulled into the drive honking the horn on Samuel's new Chevrolet automobile. Molly and I rushed out to see what was making all that racket.

Molly nearly jumped out of her skin when Samuel again blew the horn as she walked in front of the vehicle to greet Crawford. "Yikes, I thought it was going to get me, Crawford. You need to tame down that friend of yours," she said as she laughed and gave Crawford a squashing hug.

"I'm so glad you came. You need to spend at least a week here to rest, Crawford." I caught the look that sailed between him and Samuel, and no one said a word for a few seconds. "Come on in, now. Molly and I were just going to have a little lunch."

Crawford took my arm as the other two headed inside. "We can only stay two days." My face must have dropped. "Wait, there's a good reason. I know you're not going to like this, but Samuel and I both volunteered for duty. We need to report on the fifth."

Horror filled my insides, and I nearly doubled over with instant pain. "No, Crawford, you're too old for duty. Why would you do such a thing?"

He hugged me and I turned to rest my body against him. "I needed something to get my mind off losing Elaine and our baby. This seemed like a good way. I'm sorry it hurts you so much, though."

Making myself deal with this news, I took deep breaths as we walked arm in arm into the dining room. Molly looked up, tears in her eyes. Samuel must have told her the news. We sat down to eat quiet at first, then Samuel shared a story about their trip to Willow

Lake.

"The people in Morris sure got a laugh today. We drove through there on the way here. A lot of folks started pointing at us and laughing as we drove down the main street."

Crawford started laughing, too, and the mood began to change. "I told Samuel to stop so we could figure out what was so funny. When we got out and walked around the auto, there on the front below the radiator was stuck a big 'ole hen, pierced through by the rod that holds the hand crank."

At that, Samuel broke into such a raucous laugh, he could hardly finish the story. Molly and I looked at one another and couldn't help but join in the infectious merriment.

"On our trip here today, as we rounded a curve in the road, a flock of chickens filled the roadway. I got so excited, instead of stepping on the brake, I stomped on the gas and the fowl dispersed every which way, some flying over the car. One unlucky fowl committed suicide today."

Wiping away my tears from the high spirits, I felt some relief from the news of Crawford's enlistment. Putting that news in the back of my mind, I vowed to enjoy the next two days with my son and Samuel. "So, what are your plans for the next two days, deer hunting?"

Crawford smirked. "That sounds great, as long as you promise not to come along."

My hands shoved up the weight of the air in disbelief. "I can't help it those deer are so scared of me."

To Samuel, Crawford explained, "Mom goes through the woods whistling and humming and it makes it almost impossible to get a deer with all that racket. I think she's on the side of the deer."

By the time we had finished off our evening in the parlor enjoying a couple glasses of wine, I had nearly forgotten about Crawford's news. That is, until retiring for the evening, and was left alone in my room. After tossing about for several hours before falling asleep, I didn't wake early enough to accompany the hunters. When they returned about noon, sure enough, a large deer sprawled across the back of the buckboard.

Hanging the carcass from the barn rafters, I watched as the two city slickers gutted the deer. "Cut some of that meat into strips and Molly and I will show you how to make jerky out of it. When you come back from that blasted war, it'll be all ready to eat."

For the next day and a half, Crawford, Samuel and I spent our time preparing the meat strips for drying, riding around the farm, checking out our livestock, and visiting Morris. Arriving in town in the same vehicle that had previously been a source of derision prompted another wave of individuals recounting the incident involving the impaled chicken. We couldn't help but join in the laughing.

When we returned to the house, another horse and rider had arrived. The large man introduced himself as the newly appointed game warden for the county, Jacob Roberts.

He shook our hands, and I thought it best to be on the good side of this officer. "Nice to meet you. We were just going in to have some coffee and biscuits. Come on in and join us, won't you?"

Settling around the table in Molly's kitchen, we laughed again at the chicken story. Mr. Roberts joined the festive spirit. When all quieted down, he said, "I'm on the lookout for deer poachers. The season doesn't start until the third week of October."

The room fell silent. He looked around the table at our now downcast faces. "From the guilty looks on your faces, guess I need to arrest all of you for killing deer out of season."

I stood and paced the length of the room. "Well, warden, we weren't aware of any deer season. We've always shot deer at Willow Lake whenever the need arose. These young city guys are leaving for war soon, so I shot a deer yesterday so Molly could cook the venison for a nice meal before they go. Guess you must have smelled the jerky being cured in the smokehouse."

"Mom don't lie for us." Crawford stood and put his arm around me. "Samuel and I shot that deer, Mr. Roberts."

The warden's face broke into a broad smile, his laugh filled the room, and he slapped his knee. "I was just having a little fun with you. I had no idea you shot a deer." We all sighed, relieved to be off the hook. Then, all traces of mirth left the game warden's face. "Guess nobody shot a deer in my book. You boys need to take care of yourselves over there in Europe, you hear? I know from experience. War's no picnic. I fought in Cuba during the Spanish-American War."

That explained why Mr. Roberts was still working as a warden at his age.

Mr. Roberts needed to continue his rounds, so both boys shook his hand, and walked him to the door, no doubt getting more advice on staying safe.

~

I shall always remember the morning when the long buff-colored envelope came by the early post. Molly answered the knock at the door with me only steps behind. Handing it to me, I sat down before opening it. My face froze as stiff as a mask as I read the post. I handed the letter to Molly, saying in a quiet voice, "Crawford is dead. He was killed in France."

My life spiraled out of control. How could I go on without George and now Crawford? I felt myself sink into the mire of despair. Staying in bed till all hours in the morning became my way of coping. Poor Josiah was left to run the homestead. I didn't even want to come down when he needed advice.

Finally in November, the word spread through the countryside that the Armistice was signed on the eleventh hour of the eleventh day of the eleventh month. Crawford's enlistment occurred just before this event, rendering his death unnecessary. If only he had waited to enlist, he'd be returning home to me alive instead of in a casket.

Chapter 24

Bailey feared Josie wouldn't be able to finish her story. She could see her aunt becoming weaker as the days passed. Often Josie didn't make it down for breakfast and after sitting for only an hour or two, she would excuse herself to return to her room to lie down.

Then one Sunday afternoon in summer, Aunt Josie asked, "Do you think John would mind driving us to Willow Lake? I'd love to see the old place again."

When John came in from feeding the animals he was caring for at the office, Bailey confronted him with Josie's request. "That sounds like fun. I'd like to see it myself."

Bailey gave John a hug. "Thanks, I'll fix us a picnic lunch to take with, just in case Aunt Josie wants to stay a bit. I'm afraid the ruins will make her very sad, though. People say there's not much left of the town. We'll have to be ready to pack up quickly if she gets too upset."

Aunt Josie sat in front with John so she could get in and out of the old Chevi more easily. The wind whistling through the open windows, made it difficult for Bailey to hear. She moved forward as much as possible to hear the conversation in the front seat.

"Drive over to those crumbling blocks over there, John. That was the depot at one time. See, the tracks still pass right here."

John did as he was told and parked the car where they could have a place to sit. He set up the folding chair for Josie and he and Bailey sat on a blanket in front of her. Bailey unpacked the basket, but before they could start to eat, Aunt Josie started in again on her story.

1919-1920

It took me quite a while to get over Crawford's passing, but life has a way of moving on even if we don't want it to. Josiah had a lot to do with me recovering from my depression. Every day at dinner, he stopped by to give me a report of the day's activities. Hearing how my hogs and cattle were flourishing without me, piqued my interest and I started to become curious about whether Josiah was embellishing about how well everything was going.

"Tomorrow morning, stop by around ten o'clock. I want to check for myself how well the farm is doing."

The sun shone brightly on a new dusting of snow as Josiah, and I bundled up and drove from one area
of Willow Lake to another. It was as Josiah said, everything seemed to be running smoothly. I started to come alive inside again as I watched the hired hands feed the pigs and toss plenty of hay to the horses.

"Everything looks great, Josiah, but let's get together again tomorrow and go over the accounts. Then I can really see whether anything needs to be dealt with."

When I came down the next morning, I walked right into the kitchen like I always did without announcing myself and got the biggest surprise. There stood Molly and Josiah in one another's arms. "Oh, my, excuse me. I didn't realize, um, sorry, um, I'll leave you two alone."

Red faced, Molly and Josiah parted, but their hands stayed clasped. "Don't leave. I'm so glad this is finally out in the open. I'm tired of trying to keep this a secret." Molly's smile lit up her face when she looked from me to Josiah.

"With you down in the dumps, we didn't feel right about being so happy, so we decided to wait before telling you. Molly and I would love to have your blessing to get married soon. Neither of us is getting any younger." Josiah stopped to take a breath, "Maybe we could have a Christmas wedding."

"Well, let's go over the accounts and then get this wedding planned. What better way to celebrate Christmas than with a wedding."

Josiah and Molly decided to get married in the small church in Morris, and the house at Willow Lake would be opened for guests for both a huge Christmas celebration and the merriment of their wedding. At least using the wine from our cellar would still be legal. The government had ratified the Eighteenth amendment authorizing Prohibition, but it would not go into effect until Jan. 17, 1920.

I did not understand the motivation behind the Woman's Christian Temperance Union. They had the idea that alcohol was a scourge on society and that its prohibition would lead to a more moral and prosperous America. Even though I had experienced Charles' uncontrolled drinking, my thought was, a drink occasionally, as long as in moderation, wouldn't hurt anyone. I had spent the majority of my life in that manner.

Decorating for the celebration provided a distraction from my mourning. The greenery we used as swag throughout the house and the pinecones we added here and there, gave the rooms the wonderfully fresh scent of pine. Carriage lanterns cast shimmering lights throughout the parlor, dining room, foyer and library. A beautiful pine tree decorated with popcorn strings, paper chains, and tinsel icicles adorned the large foyer. Although electric lights now lit the town of Morris, at the homestead we still did not have that luxury, so candles mounted on the branches brought a warm, flickering light to the tree.

On the day of the wedding the happy couple enjoyed a very private ceremony with only Caleb, Josiah's right-hand man and me in attendance. Later in the afternoon, Josiah and Molly greeted the wedding guests at my home and directed them to the many food items laid out in the dining room. Wine began to flow and because of the imminent prohibition of spirits, the discussion turned to the new law.

"They can't stop us from using up what we have stashed away. It's ours to keep and enjoy in the privacy of our homes.," said one guest.

"The law only says we can't manufacture, sell or transport the stuff. Guess we can still drink it," added another guest.

My ears opened when I heard another man expound about the making of spirits. "The law's unclear about making wine at home. Home stills might be illegal, but you can still purchase them at some hardware stores. I even saw a pamphlet the other day at the library with instructions on how to make wine."

The group laughed and the same man continued. "They think they'll make us into teetotalers, but instead we'll become law breakers."

My mind started mulling over their comments. Perhaps during the cold, dark days of January, making my own spirits would be something I could do to keep me focused and from dwelling on the past. Never being a person to have someone tell me I couldn't do something; I began collecting the items I needed to brew my own alcohol. Josiah found and purchased a copper still from a neighbor's barn that had belonged to a long ago grandfather and hadn't been used recently. I visited the library in Rensselaer and checked out books on home brewing. Once the weather improved, Josiah helped me set the still up towards the back of the hog woodlands where no one would think to look.

We had to be careful because the warden, Jacob Roberts, had begun stopping by whenever he traveled through our area. Josiah started teasing me. "Jacob can't be just checking for stills all the time. Mark my words, Josie, he's interested in courting you."

He laughed when he said this, but was there some truth to it? This relationship never occurred to me until Josiah commented. I needed to be careful about how I treated Jacob in the future. While I enjoyed his visits, I never again wanted to get close enough to someone to have to mourn their passing.

After siphoning off a batch of apricot brandy earlier at the still site, I drove up to the front of the house. Climbing down from the buckboard, I nearly jumped to the heavens at the sight of a handsome guy standing by the hitching rail. I glanced back to make sure the spirits were covered well with the canvas. Having the keg so close to an officer of the law could be a disaster. I didn't know for sure whether Jacob would report my small still, but I didn't want to find out.

"Thought I'd stop by since I was in the area. Got time to sit for a spell?" Jacob tied his horse and walked toward me. I gave him a quick hug and guided him toward the walkway to the house.

"Come on in. I'll have Molly make us some tea. Go on in the parlor. I need to change into something more presentable." Placing my Winchester on the foyer table, I went upstairs and changed from my baggy jeans and plaid shirt that smelled of alcohol to a comfortable homespun dress with a satin belt.

Jacob stood by the empty fireplace staring down at the spent ashes. His bare arms were sun-speckled and leathery from years of exposure to the wind and weather. His silver-grey hair, cropped short, and his straight nose and high cheek bones gave him an air of nobility. When I tapped him on the shoulder, he turned and gave me the most disarming smile. I began to wonder if I could hold him at arm's length much longer or if I even wanted to.

We sat together on the settee and Jacob took my hand in his. "Got two things to ask you about."

Looking down, I straightened the fabric of my dress with my left hand, hoping he was not going to ask me to marry him. "Well, go on then. Don't keep it bottled in."

"You don't know who has been working that still on your property, do you? Someone reported the smell of boiling mash and noticed a thin line of smoke back there in your hog patch."

The temperature of my body rose and sweat formed on my upper lip and forehead. I pulled my hand from his to wipe both. Jacob turned my face toward him, with his now free hand. When I raised my eyes to meet his, I could tell. He knew it was my still.

"Oh, Josie, don't you know how dangerous those things are? I won't turn you in, but you must promise me you'll dismantle it and stop this foolishness."

I could see how much he cared for me in that instant and I feared the second thing he wanted to ask.

Trying to make light of the serious issue, I laughed and said, "If you're that worried about it, I promise I'll get rid of it. I don't want someone else to come along to turn me in and I'd have to spend my last days in jail. Besides, I already have plenty of brew." Again, I chuckled, but Jacob's face remained serious. I wanted to get this over with, so I asked, "Now what's the second thing you wanted to say?"

He looked away for a second and took a breath. "They've reassigned me to Chicago. What with all the moonshining going on, they want more guys in the city to weed it out. I think you know how I feel about you." He paused and smiled. "Josie, do you think you could see your way clear to go with me as my wife?"

Chapter 25

John and Bailey had hung on every word, but now the late afternoon sun reminded them they needed to get Aunt Josie home. She had done better than Bailey had imagined. The wreckage of the town had not bothered her as much as Bailey had thought it would.

On the ride home, Aunt Josie's eyes scanned what was left of her town. "Such a shame. We worked so hard to make Morris a viable town. I know now it was too close to Laketown to sustain growth. It had to be one or the other to succeed and Laketown won out."

Before long Josie's head bobbed against the back of the seat. She had fallen asleep after all the excitement of returning to her town. Bailey and John rode along in silence back to their house, keeping their thoughts to themselves. Stopping the car in the driveway, Aunt Josie woke. "Oh, we're back home already? You know, Bailey, there's not too much more to tell about my life. Would you like to finish after we've had a chance to freshen up?"

"Mind if I sit in?" asked John. "I've been reading all of Bailey's newspaper stories, so I feel like I'm invested in knowing how it ends."

Josie laughed. "John, you already know how it will end."

John's quizzical face searched Bailey's as if to say, what's she talking about?

Calling back, she explained, "She means we'll be dealing with her until her passing." Bailey hurried to the lavatory, hoping her monthly visitor had not made its appearance.

When all three had settled in the parlor, Josie continued where she had left off.

1920-1930's

Obviously, I did not go to Chicago with Jacob, but he continued to return to Willow Lake regularly, at first. As will often happen when miles separate a relationship, Jacob eventually found someone else in Chicago and they married. I was happy for him and Edith. He deserved a devoted wife, although Edith was one of those involved in The League of Women Voters, so I'm not sure she knew how to love a man like Jacob. The League had been influential in getting the 19th amendment passed. When it took effect, women were given the right to vote. Although I stood behind what these women did, I kept out of groups like these. Willow Lake and Morris gave me more than enough to do.

Ultimately, my financial difficulties were due to obtaining the incentive loans with provisions for low interest, I had borrowed several years previous. The loans were designed to help farmers increase production which we had done, but before long the loans needed to be repaid, and I didn't have the money. I was land and property rich; but I didn't have the cash flow needed. I had no other tactic than to start selling off some of my property. By the year 1925, my seven thousand acres had dwindled to sixteen hundred acres, all still heavily mortgaged.

Josiah stopped each morning as he always had. Molly no longer ran my household chores. She and Josiah had purchased a home in Morris, and I hired a young woman from town to take her place. Nothing remained the same and my disposition became even more cranky at times. I looked forward to the days when Molly accompanied Josiah back to the homestead, but today he drove up by himself in the Ford Model T truck I had purchased for his use.

Without a salutation, he started in. "Got a couple more people unable to keep up their rent on their farm, so they're packing up and moving to the city to get jobs. They say they can make more money working in a factory. If we don't do something, there's not going to be anyone left."

"I don't know what else to do. I've sold off a good portion of my property and most of the livestock. It's those high prices we've been paying for feed and getting no return when we send the animals to the market. Congress keeps passing bills that are supposedly going to help, but I haven't seen any yet."

"I'll be having the boys round up the few cattle that are left for shipment next week. That should bring in a little money."

"Yeah, and after that, you'll have to let most of those hired hands go. I don't have the money to pay them anymore."

Nothing we tried seemed to help get us back on track. More and more of the farm renters left for the city and the lower population on the farms caused businesses to close in the town of Morris. It became a vicious cycle with no way to stop it. By 1930, they were calling what was happening, The Great Depression. My town of Morris was so deserted, people called it a ghost town. The railroad ceased its journey into the town and many of the buildings became broken shells of their former beauty. More of my property was divided and sold to pay the mortgages. I made sure Josiah and Molly retained an income, but Josiah's arthritis kept him from doing many chores. Molly often came to visit. We'd always gravitate toward the kitchen table. Molly felt most comfortable there in the place where she had created so many delicious dishes for many years.

I made the tea for us and laid out the cookies Susan had baked. "She'll never live up to your cooking and baking, but she's okay to have around. She's busy cleaning so we can have some peace for a bit."

Molly loved to share all the news she had heard when she visited. "I read just yesterday; four bandits held up the Lowell National Bank. They fired shots into the floor and got away with five thousand dollars. I bet it was that Dillinger gang."

"If it was, that fat sheriff will never catch them." We laughed, but then I had to ask. "I hear the pastor decided to close the church in Morris. Where will we go for our service now? I just can't abide going to Laketown."

Molly touched my arm. She knew why I felt that way. "Maybe in nice weather we could drive to Rensselaer. It's not that far in these new automobiles." Continuing to rub my arm, her concern became unmistakable. "Josie, are you feeling, okay? Your color just isn't good lately."

"I must admit, I'm just not up to doing much anymore. The pain in my joints keeps me from working like I should."

The next week when Josiah came by, he found me on the floor of the barn. My old horse didn't mean it, but he skittered left as I brushed his coat. He knocked me over and I just couldn't pull myself up. Poor Josiah. He was beside himself. The other hired hands had moved on years ago, so he had no one to help get me up.

"Just hold on here, Josie. I'll move the truck closer to the door and go get Susan to help me."

He was gone before I could tell him I needed to use the chamber pot first. It was all so embarrassing. By the time they came back I was sitting in my own urine. "Josiah, please go back to the truck and wait. Susan, could you please bring me some clean clothes." I hadn't lost my will to live, only my dignity.

Once I was cleaned up a bit, they managed to load me up and take me to Jasper County Hospital. I broke my hip in September, and stayed in the hospital for almost a month. They put me in some kind of contraption called hip traction. During that month, Molly and Josiah took care of selling off the last of my property to pay the hospital bill.

~

"That's about where you and John came into my life, and I will forever be grateful for your kindness in taking me in. The doctors told me I could no longer live on my own. It was either move in with you and John or go to a county home."

"I'm just glad I heard from one of the nurses at the hospital that you were there," said Bailey. "Mom always told me stories about my Great Aunt Josie, but for some reason, we never visited you."

Josie stared down at her hands. "Well, this is one of those stories referred to as the elephant in the room."

With furrowed brow, Bailey looked at John. "What are you talking about?"

Josie hesitated, then continued, head down. "In those days, everyone covered up their mistakes. Well, Crawford made a big one when he was in college. He had a child before he married Elaine. I agreed to support the mother and child until the boy turned eighteen, but we never kept in touch other than with the money that I sent."

Bailey stood and paced. "So, how are we related then?" She looked to John for help.

"I'm not really your great aunt, I'm your great grandmother, through the son Crawford had. That's why your family never spoke much about me except with derogatory stories. I'm so sorry I did not claim my grandson after Crawford died, but I was afraid he wouldn't accept me. It's another regret I have to deal with in my life."

John came to Bailey and held her in a side hug. "Even better, Bailey. She's just a little closer family than you first thought. I did often wonder how she could be your aunt when Crawford was her only child, but I didn't want to bring it up."

Josie picked up her hanky and wiped her eyes. "I don't care what you call me, Bailey. I'm just happy to be here with you in my last years."

Bailey's face lit up. "If it's alright with you, I think I'll still call you, Aunt Josie. It's how I've always thought of you." Bailey hugged Josie, acknowledging their new family connection. "Now, how about we eat the rest of that picnic lunch I made? Come into the kitchen so we can sit at a table this time."

Epilogue

John and Bailey continued to care for Josie at their home until she died peacefully on October 14, 1939. They buried her beside her beloved husband, George, in the Mound Grove Cemetery in Kankakee. Josie was eighty-three.

Bailey's last newspaper story included an obituary for her Aunt Josie. The previous stories had not mentioned Josie by name, but this time Bailey wanted people to know it was Josie she had been writing about. She felt Josie would forgive her for identifying her now that she was gone.

Josie (Riley) Morris was born to Margaret and Henry Riley in 1856. She had one son, Crawford who was killed in 1918 in WW I. She married the love of her life, George Morris, in Rensselaer in 1887. George and Josie moved back to Willow Lake in 1888 where they built their home. She was preceded in death by her mother, father, first husband, James McKnight, husband, George Morris, son Crawford and daughter-in-law, Elaine. Determined to make her business successful, Josie divided her farm into smaller units to rent to individuals. In 1908, Josie received permission to build her town of Morris which included a stockyard with a capacity of 5000 head of cattle, a block plant, hotel, railway stations, a combination general store and post office, church, school, a central park and cottages for employees. She gradually specialized in the raising of Spotted Poland-China hogs, eventually having the largest

herd of any breeder in the association, establishing herself as one of the major livestock producers in northern Indiana. Josie died in her sleep on October 14, 1939, at the home of her niece.

Bailey did not enter her aunt's room again until a week after they had discovered her still body, gone in her sleep. When she did go in again, it struck Bailey as one of the saddest things she had ever seen. The room was bare of embellishments. It wouldn't take long to clean it out. The meagre amount of clothing in the wardrobe and in the bureau drawers did not point to the wealth that Josie had once enjoyed.

Bailey stripped the bed for laundering and started packing the few pieces of clothing into a box that she would probably donate to the church's rummage sale. Next, she opened the bureau drawers to empty them. Some items like worn underthings and broken jewelry, she tossed into a bag for the garbage. She kept the antique handkerchiefs for herself to remember her aunt, but the shawls, sweaters and costume jewelry she packed in with her aunt's dresses for the church sale. Josie had already given Bailey her rings and diamond earrings she always wore, so Bailey figured those were the only things of value her aunt possessed. Pulling out the items in the bottom drawer, Bailey felt a small box in the back of the space. She pulled it out to examine it. The expensive looking wood bore the carved inscription, 'Mom, Love Crawford.' Could this be the same small box Josie had mentioned in her story?

Bailey tried opening the lid, but the lock held it tight. She would have to wait until John came in.

She carried all the items down to the middle of the kitchen and set the ones for the church in the corner for later. The mysterious box and hankies she displayed on the dining room table for when John returned after work. Sitting down at the table, she stared blankly, imagining what could be in the box. Would the five gold coins be in there?

When John came through the back door after work, he called, "Where's my beautiful wife?"

"In here. You might want to bring some small tools, too."

Bailey got up to give John a hug and pointed to the cache on the table. He whistled when he saw the box and his eyes widened. "You don't suppose that's the same box Josie talked about in her story, do you?"

"I've been thinking about it. She never mentioned the gold pieces again after she got them appraised. Maybe it could be THE same box. But it's locked and I didn't find a key while going through her things."

John started using the small tools to try to pry the box open, but it wouldn't budge. "Did you check under the drawers. I've heard of people taping keys to the bottom of drawers."

Both took off for the stairway, pulling each other back so the other could go ahead while nearly doubling over with laughter. John managed to enter the room first and started pulling the drawers out, checking under each as he did.

Bailey entered just as he pulled out the bottom drawer. "That's where I found the box."

Turning it over, sure enough, the key was taped to the bottom. Bailey grabbed it and ran out of the room, skipping every other step going down. She could hear John breathing right behind her. They both paused in front of the small ornate box to assess their actions.

Bailey looked into John's eyes. "We're acting too crazy. It's like we have gold fever."

"I know. We need to slow down and think about this. Even if the gold coins are in the box, we might not be able to keep them. What about her estate?"

"There is no estate, John. That's why we ended up taking care of Josie. I'm going to open the box and then we'll worry about the contents, if there is anything."

Her hand shook as she placed the tiny key into the lock. Turning it a quarter turn to the right, the lid popped up a bit. Squeezing her eyes shut, Bailey lifted the lid like she might open a heavy door. When she heard John gasp, she opened her eyes. Five small gold coins lay on the bottom of the velvet lining. Taking them out one by one, they placed them on the table. Underneath two of the coins was a small, folded piece of paper. Bailey lifted it and opened it with care, trying not to show her excitement.

"It's a letter and it's addressed to us."

"Let me see." John grabbed it from Bailey, nearly tearing it in two. He held it high so Bailey couldn't reach it.

Both laughing, Bailey jumped up to reach it as John tickled her belly. She gave up. "Okay you can read it to me."

Dear John and Bailey,

I am leaving these five gold pieces to the two of you. The last time I checked, they were not worth much, but they may be worth more in the future. Do whatever you wish to do with them. The only thing I ask is that you don't let them drive a wedge between you two. You are such a devoted couple. I would hate to think I had done anything to cause a rift. Thank you again for taking me into your home. You have restored my view of loving relationships. At one time I thought finding Shatner's gold would make me happy. Far from it. The love for others that comes from our Savior is the only true happiness in this life. I hope the coins will help with the care of that baby that is coming soon.
Yours, Aunt Josie

When John finished reading, he looked up at Bailey. "Baby? What's she talking about?"

Bailey's face held a sheepish grin. "I don't know how she knew. I wasn't sure myself until a few days ago, but yes, we're having a baby."

John dropped the letter and grabbed Bailey, smothering her with kisses. Holding her at arm's length, he looked down to check out her tummy. Laughing, John, looked up expecting Bailey to be laughing along with him.

But instead, Bailey's eyes filled with crocodile tears. "John, I'm so glad we invited Aunt Josie to live with us. Not because of the gold, but because she had no one. Molly and Josiah are her only friends left, but they're barely able to care for themselves anymore. It was the right thing to do. Staying here helped her to die with dignity. Thank you for helping me to do this for her."

Bailey threw her arms around John again. "Guess we need to get that gold appraised so we can start on the nursery."

1948

"Come here, Ryder. Come here, old boy. Where'd you take off to?"

Snow covered the small tree-covered hill as Bobby followed behind his excited beagle. During Christmas break, he and Ryder came out to hunt rabbits whenever they could get away. Chores had to be done first, of course.

Bobby caught up with Ryder where several large oak trees grew in a cluster. Ryder had followed a rabbit's scent, but the ground beneath the oaks was a maze of tracks made by other rabbits earlier that morning. Ryder had become distracted. Instead of sniffing out an animal, Ryder was digging with all his might.

"What's in there, boy? Hmmm? What's you got?"

Bobby pulled him off. A wooden lid encircled by a rusted metal ring protruded from the ground. Bobby first used his foot to dig deeper, then got down on his knees to dig around the shape with his gloved hands. The cold dirt didn't respond well to digging. So, he grabbed a large stick and dug a little deeper.

"Hey, could be treasure, Ryder. In school I read about this guy who buried a nail keg full of gold."

Once enough dirt had been cleared away from the top, Bobby lifted the lid and peered inside. Reaching in for the anticipated gold, some useless metal objects filled his hands, springs, nails, washers, nuts and bolts. Disappointment filled his whole frame.

"Well, Ryder, guess we better stick to rabbit hunting. Come on. Go get the scent."

Author's Notes

LOVED AND LOST is very loosely patterned after the life of Jennie Conrad. As I looked for a woman to emulate for this historical novel about the settlement of northwest Indiana, Jennie's life came forward as an interesting female character to imitate. I used the timeline of her life and some of the historical events she knew about. However, most of the events and some of the place names are completely fictional and in no way are they meant to be an actual account of Jennie Conrad's life.

According to Richard C. Schmal from an article in the June 27, 1990, Lowell Tribune, Jennie M. Conrad became a legend in her own lifetime, with she and her family drastically transforming Newton County by draining Beaver Lake. Jennie married George Conrad when she was twenty-three in 1878, and their son, Platt Conrad, was born in 1880. The family moved to Indiana from Chicago in 1891. George died suddenly on Aug. 11, 1896, at the age of fifty-eight, leaving Jennie a widow at age forty-one, when her son was only sixteen years old. She decided that the practical thing to do was to make do with what she had, and she was determined to succeed as a woman entrepreneur. In about 1915 she wrote describing her farm: "Oak Dene Farm contains five thousand acres, and when sufficient laborers are available it is about three quarters under cultivation with wheat, rye, corn, oats, clover, alfalfa and timothy and the balance of the land is in blue grass pastures with some oak woodlands made hog-tight, permitting the gleaning of the acorn crop. In autumn it is customary to allow the hogs to live on blue grass and acorns for two months. Nearly all the pastures have running water. Early in my occupancy I began to fill the place with an improved class of livestock, with a view of feeding them all farm products, a system still in existence." She was especially proud of her hogs, and rightly so.

Around the turn of the century, Jennie was running another profitable business, boarding horses for her friends in Chicago, many of them well known in finance and business circles in the city.

It was practical for Jennie to plan the Town of Conrad. She needed a place nearby to ship her cattle, produce, and manufactured items to the market in Chicago. Before that time, her cattle were herded to Roselawn and shipped on the Monon Railroad. Her little village included a church, post office, a school, the stock yards and cottages for the employees. Railroad sidings were built for the stock yard and for the cement block factory. Jennie donated four miles of right-of-way, one hundred feet wide, to the Chicago, Indiana, and Southern Railroad (now New York Central), and she built the only stone station on the line. The stockyards had a capacity of five thousand head of cattle, and thousands were sent to the city from the Conrad location, saving the long trek to Roselawn. The block plant, located on Jane St., west of the railroad and south of the town produced blocks and can be found in buildings at Lake Village, Morocco and in cities throughout the country, including New York City. Another railroad spur was to go to a planned glass factory, but this did not come about.

Starting in the year 1885, several fateful events occurred in the city of Kankakee. Jennie had a stepmother twenty-three years younger than herself, and a very young half-sister, Mary Milk Barton. Her father died in 1893, leaving everything to the widow and his younger daughter. Her only son, Platt Conrad, left to enter the insurance business in Chicago, Ill., and there were no grandchildren.

Jennie Conrad's seven thousand acres dwindled down to sixteen hundred, all heavily mortgaged. She died in 1939, at the home of a relative in Rensselaer, and was buried beside her husband in the Mound Grove Cemetery at Kankakee. Some of the buildings in the ghost town of Conrad were still standing in the 1930's, but now all that remains of Jennie M. Conrad's dream are a few broken foundations and some lonely narrow streets in an area covered with underbrush. Her career was a legend even when she lived, and her story will carry on in history for years to come.

Gerald Born, a Newton County historian who now lives in Hammond, wrote "The Saga of Jennie Conrad," a story serialized in an area newspaper in 1988. Born wrote: "Whatever the world may think of Jennie M., we must credit her with being where the action was and for taking a large section of the state and transforming it into farmland and making it productive. And what of the town she built? It would not surprise me if someday soon, like the fabled village of Brigadoon, it may once again appear, complete with the sound of the church bell pealing and the laughter of the children playing in the school yard. One does not have to stretch the imagination very much to see that Conrad lies on the path of urbanization that is once again changing the face of the landscape in its inevitable march."

Of course, this prediction did not come true. In December 1996, The Nature Conservancy purchased seven thousand two hundred acres of agricultural ground in Newton County and began the process of converting these acres to the diverse prairies of today's Kankakee Sands. Further back in history, the land that is now Kankakee Sands was once part of the Grand Kankakee Marsh system and the home of Beaver Lake, then the largest lake in Indiana—seven miles long and five miles wide. It was a shallow lake, only ten feet at its deepest, filled with vegetation and wildlife. In 1997, the work to convert the agricultural fields to prairie began. Much historical research was done to understand the complicated prairie systems that would have historically existed and the plants that would have been a part of those prairies. More than six hundred species of plants are native to the area, and those species are used to revegetate the land of Kankakee Sands.

Today if you visit Kankakee Sands, you can begin your visit at the Visitor Kiosk in front of the Kankakee Sands office for current news and activities. Then set off to visit the Bison Viewing Area, the Birding Overlook, or one of several trails. Within Kankakee Sands you can also visit Conrad Station Savanna, a 360-acre sand savanna with black and white oaks growing on rolling sand hills and a prairie restoration planting in the southern flat ground. Along the two-mile trail through Conrad Station Savanna is an informational sign about Jennie M. Conrad, telling about the historic town of Conrad, platted in 1908.

One wonders what Jennie would say about the changes that have been made to the property she so loved and worked so diligently to develop. Would she approve of the work to transform it back to its original state? Knowing what we've learned about her industry and business sense, my feeling is, she would have tried to block the restoration work so she could build hog barns, but of course we'll never know that for sure.

BIBLIOGRAPHY

Evening Republican, Volume 59, Number 72,Rensselaer, Jasper County, 16 April 1917,Serialized in the Morocco Courier in 1989, "The Saga of Jennie M. Conrad" by Gerald Born

History of Jasper County, Indiana, 1985

Isaacs, Marion, The Kankakee River of History, 1960, Internet Archive R.

Nichols, Fay Folsom, The Kankakee: Chronicle of an Indiana River and its Fabled ,Marshes, 1965, T. Gaus & Sons T.

Pioneer History by Richard C. Schmal, Mysterious Beaver Lake, (from the May 31, 2005, Lowell Tribune, page 4)

Pioneer History by Richard C. Schmal, More About Conrad, the Ghost Town,(from the June 27, 1990, Lowell Tribune, page 10)June 27, 1990, Lowell Tribune, page 10

Pioneer History by Richard C. Schmal, The Ghost Town of Northwest Indiana, (from the May 30, 1990, Lowell Tribune, page 12)

Reed, Tales of the Vanishing River, 1920, New York: John Lane Company
Sketches of Jasper County by Beulah Arnott

Swierenga, Robert P., Publications, Dutch Immigrant Murderers Go to the Gallows, 2010

https://www.nature.org/en-us/get-involved/how-to-help/places-we-protect/conrad-station-savanna/ Paid Visit to Ranch Of Mrs. Jennie Conrad.

https://www.youtube.com/watch?v=S2SHWHKyOmI, The History of Conrad, Indiana's Forgotten Ghost Town, Mary Kay Emmrich

Janeen Swart is a teacher by profession, mother and grandmother by loving choice, and a secretary and gopher when needed. Having the goal of becoming a writer after retiring, Janeen took a writing course at Indiana University NW. She also took two correspondence courses from The Institute of Children's Literature. Her first published book was through Lighthouse Christian Publishing, A DOG AND A BOY. Later a YA book, THE HIDDEN TRUTH was published by Soul Mate Publishing and an adult fiction book was published by Winged Publications, A VISIT HOME. Janeen also has several self-published books listed on Amazon.

Dear readers,

I hope you enjoyed LOVED AND LOST. Please write an honest review on Amazon and if you're a member of Goodreads a review there would also be appreciated. Check out my other books at my website: https://janeenswart.wordpress.com.

OTHER ADULT BOOKS BY JANEEN SWART
The Hidden Truth
Going Home to the Kankakee Marsh
Memories, Moments and Musings
A Visit Hoeme
CHILDREN'S BOOKS BY JANEEN SWART
How to Be a Lady
How to Be a Super Man
A Dog and His Boy
The Bossy Beast
'Twas the Last Sop Before Christmas
Evan's Prayers
Nighttime Prowler
Secrets of Cub Creek
Christmas in Little Village